FIDELITY

Also by Wendell Berry

FICTION

The Discovery of Kentucky
The Memory of Old Jack
Nathan Coulter
A Place on Earth
Remembering
The Wild Birds

POETRY

Clearing
Collected Poems: 1957–1982
The Country of Marriage
Farming: A Hand Book
Openings
A Part: Poems
Sabbaths
Sayings and Doings
Traveling at Home
The Wheel

ESSAYS

A Continuous Harmony
The Gift of Good Land
Harlan Hubbard: Life and Work
The Hidden Wound
Home Economics
Recollected Essays: 1965–1980
Standing by Words: Essays
The Unforseen Wilderness
The Unsettling of America
What Are People For?

FIDELITY

Five Stories

Wendell Berry

PANTHEON BOOKS

NEW YORK AND SAN FRANCISCO

I thank the people who have helped me with these stories:
John and Carol Berry, Don Wallis, Donald Hall, Alison
Macondray, Nancy Palmer Jones, Jack Shoemaker,
Dominique Gioia, Tanya Berry.

I am indebted also to the editors who have previously
published these stories:

"Pray Without Ceasing" originally published in *The Southern
Review*, Fall 1992 · "A Jonquil for Mary Penn" originally
published in *The Atlantic Monthly*, February 1992 · "Making
It Home" originally published as "Homecoming" in *The
Sewanee Review*, Winter 1992 · "Fidelity" originally published
in *Orion*, Summer 1992 · "Are You All Right?" originally
published in *Wendell Berry*, Vol. IV in the Confluence American
Author Series, edited by Paul Merchant. Copyright © 1991 by
Wendell Berry.

Library of Congress Cataloging-in-Publication Data

Berry, Wendell, 1934–
Fidelity : five stories / Wendell Berry.
p. cm.
ISBN 0-679-41633-1
I. Title.
PS3552.E75F49   1992
813'.54—dc20   92–7139

Illustration by M. Kristen Bearse
Book design by Maura Fadden Rosenthal
Manufactured in the United States of America
2 4 6 8 9 7 5 3

CONTENTS

For Carol and John

FIDELITY

Pray Without Ceasing

Mat Feltner was my grandfather on my mother's side. Saying it thus, I force myself to reckon again with the strangeness of that verb *was*. The man of whom I once was pleased to say, "He is my grandfather," has become the dead man who was my grandfather. He was, and is no more. And this is a part of the great mystery we call time.

But the past is present also. And this, I think, is a part of the greater mystery we call eternity. Though Mat Feltner has been dead for twenty-five years, and I am now older than he was when I was born and have grandchildren of my own, I know his hands, their way of holding a hammer or a hoe or a set of checklines, as well as I know my own. I know his way of talking, his way of cocking his head when he began a story, the smoking pipe stem held an inch from his lips. I have in my mind, not just as a memory but as a consolation, his welcome to me when I returned home from the university and, later, from jobs in distant cities. When I sat down beside him, his hand would clap lightly onto my leg above the knee; my absence might have lasted many months, but he would say as though we had been together the day before, "Hello, Andy." The shape of his hand is printed on the flesh of my thigh as vividly as a birthmark. This man who was my grandfather is present in me, as I felt always his father to be present in him. His father was Ben. The known history of the Feltners in Port William begins with Ben.

But even the unknown past is present in us, its silence as persistent as a ringing in the ears. When I stand in the road that passes through Port William, I am standing on the strata of my history that go down through the known past into the unknown: the blacktop rests on state gravel, which rests on county gravel, which rests on the creek rock and cinders laid down by the town when it was still mostly beyond the reach of the county; and under the creek rock and cinders is the dirt track of the town's beginning, the buffalo trace that was the way we came. You work your way down, or not so much down as within, into the interior of the present, until finally you come to that beginning in which all things, the world and the light itself, at a word welled up into being out of their absence. And nothing is here that we are beyond the reach of merely because we do not know about it. It

4

is always the first morning of Creation and always the last day, always the now that is in time and the Now that is not, that has filled time with reminders of Itself.

When my grandfather was dying, I was not thinking about the past. My grandfather was still a man I knew, but as he subsided day by day he was ceasing to be the man I had known. I was experiencing consciously for the first time that transformation in which the living, by dying, pass into the living, and I was full of grief and love and wonder.

And so when I came out of the house one morning after breakfast and found Braymer Hardy sitting in his pickup truck in front of my barn, I wasn't expecting any news. Braymer was an old friend of my father's; he was curious to see what Flora and I would do with the long-abandoned Harford Place that we had bought and were fixing up, and sometimes he visited. His way was not to go to the door and knock. He just drove in and stopped his old truck at the barn and sat looking around until somebody showed up.

"Well, you ain't much of a Catlett," he said, in perfect good humor. "Marce Catlett would have been out and gone two hours ago."

"I do my chores *before* breakfast," I said, embarrassed by the lack of evidence. My grandfather Catlett would, in fact, have been out and gone two hours ago.

"But," Braymer said in an explanatory tone, as if talking to himself, "I reckon your daddy is a late sleeper, being as he's an office man. But that Wheeler was always a shotgun once he *got* out," he went on, clearly implying, and still in excellent humor, that the family line had reached its nadir in me. "But maybe you're a right smart occupied of a night, I don't know." He raked a large cud of tobacco out of his cheek with his forefinger and spat.

He looked around with the air of a man completing an inspection, which is exactly what he was doing. "Well, it looks like you're making a little headway. You got it looking some better. Here," he said, pawing among a litter of paper, tools, and other odds and ends on top of the dashboard and then on the seat beside him, "I brought you something." He eventually forceped forth an old newspaper page folded into a tight rectangle the size of a wallet and handed it through the truck window. "You ought to have it. It ain't no good to me. The madam, you know, is hell for an antique. She bought an old desk at a sale, and that was in one of the drawers."

I unfolded the paper and read the headline: BEN FELTNER, FRIEND TO ALL, SHOT DEAD IN PORT WILLIAM.

"Ben Feltner was your great-granddaddy."

"Yes. I know."

"I remember him. He was fine as they come. They never made 'em no finer. The last man on earth you'd a thought would get shot."

"So I've heard."

"Thad Coulter was a good kind of feller, too, far as that goes. I don't reckon he was the kind you'd a thought would shoot somebody, either."

He pushed his hat back and scratched his forehead. "One of them things," he said. "They happen."

He scratched his head some more and propped his wrist on top of the steering wheel, letting the hand dangle.

"Tell you," he said, "there ain't a way in this world to know what a human creature is going to do next. I loaned a feller five hundred dollars once. He was a good feller, too, wasn't a thing wrong with him far as I knew, I liked him. And dogged if he didn't kill himself fore it was a week."

"Killed himself," I said.

"*Killed* himself," Braymer said. He meditated a moment, looking off at his memory of the fellow and wiggling two of the fingers that hung over the steering wheel. "Don't you know," he said, "not wishing him no bad luck, but I wished he'd a done it a week or two sooner."

I laughed.

"Well," he said, "I know you want to be at work. I'll get out of your way."

I said, "Don't be in a hurry," but he was starting the truck and didn't hear me. I called, "Thanks!" as he backed around. He raised his hand, not looking at me, and drove away, steering with both hands, with large deliberate motions, as if the truck were the size of a towboat.

There was an upturned feed bucket just inside the barn door. I sat down on it and unfolded the paper again. It was the front page of the Hargrave *Weekly Express*, flimsy and yellow, nearly illegible in some of the creases. It told how, on a Saturday morning in the July of 1912, Ben Feltner, who so far as was known had had no enemies, had been killed by a single shot to the head from a .22 caliber revolver. His assailant, Thad Coulter, had said, upon turning himself in to the sheriff at Hargrave soon after the incident, "I've killed the best friend I ever had." It was not a long article. It told about the interment of

Ben Feltner and named his survivors. It told nothing that I did not know, and I knew little more than it told. I knew that Thad Coulter had killed himself in jail, shortly after the murder. And I knew that he was my grandfather Catlett's first cousin.

I had learned that much, not from anyone's attempt, ever, to tell me the story, but from bits and pieces dropped out of conversations among my elders, in and out of the family. Once, for instance, I heard my mother say to my father that she had always been troubled by the thought of Thad Coulter's lonely anguish as he prepared to kill himself in the Hargrave jail. I had learned what I knew, the bare outline of the event, without asking questions, both fearing the pain that I knew surrounded the story and honoring the silence that surrounded the pain.

But sitting in the barn that morning, looking at the old page opened on my knees, I saw how incomplete the story was as the article told it and as I knew it. And seeing it so, I felt incomplete myself. I suddenly wanted to go and see my grandfather. I did not intend to question him. I had never heard him speak so much as a word about his father's death, and I could not have imagined breaking his silence. I only wanted to be in his presence, as if in his presence I could somehow enter into the presence of an agony that I knew had shaped us all.

With the paper folded again in my shirt pocket, I drove the two miles to Port William and turned in under the old maples beside the house. When I let myself in, the house was quiet, and I went as quietly as I could to my grandfather's room, thinking he might be asleep. But he was awake, his fingers laced together on top of the bedclothes. He had seen me drive in and was watching the door when I entered the room.

"Morning," I said.

He said, "Morning, son," and lifted one of his hands.

"How're you feeling?"

"Still feeling."

I sat down in the rocker by the bed and told him, in Braymer's words, the story of the too-late suicide.

My grandfather laughed. "I expect that grieved Braymer."

"Is Braymer pretty tight?" I asked, knowing he was.

"I wouldn't say 'tight,' but he'd know the history of every dollar he ever made. Braymer's done a lot of hard work."

My grandmother had heard us talking, and now she called me. "Oh, Andy!"

"I'll be back," I said, and went to see what she wanted.

She was sitting in the small bedroom by the kitchen where she had always done her sewing and where she slept now that my grandfather was ill. She was sitting by the window in the small cane-bottomed rocking chair that was her favorite. Her hands were lying on her lap and she was not rocking. I knew that her arthritis was hurting her; otherwise, at that time of day, she would have been busy at something. She had medicine for the arthritis, but it made her feel unlike herself; up to a certain point of endurability, she preferred the pain. She sat still and let the pain go its way and occupied her mind with thoughts. Or that is what she said she did. I believed, and I was as sure as if she had told me, that when she sat alone that way, hurting or not, she was praying. Though I never heard her pray aloud in my life, it seems to me now that I can reproduce in my mind the very voice of her prayers.

She had called me in to find out things, which was her way. I sat down on the stool in front of her and submitted to examination. She wanted to know what Flora was doing, and what the children were doing, and when I had seen my mother, and what she had been doing. She asked exacting questions that called for much detail in the answers, watching me intently to see that I withheld nothing. She did not tolerate secrets, even the most considerate ones. She had learned that we sometimes omitted or rearranged facts to keep her from worrying, but her objection to that was both principled and passionate. If we were worried, she wanted to worry with us; it was her place, she said.

After a while, she quit asking questions but continued to look at me. And then she said, "You're thinking about something you're not saying. What is it? Tell Granny."

She had said that to me many times in the thirty years I had known her. By then, I thought it was funny. But if I was no longer intimidated, I was still compelled. In thirty years I had never been able to deceive her when she was looking straight at me. I could have lied, but she would have known it and then would have supposed that somebody was sick. I laughed and handed her the paper out of my pocket.

"Braymer Hardy brought that to me this morning."

She unfolded it, read a little of the article but not all,

and folded it back up. Her hands lay quiet in her lap again, and she looked out the window, though obviously not seeing what was out there that morning. Another morning had come to her, and she was seeing it again through the interval of fifty-three years.

"It's a wonder," she said, "that Mat didn't kill Thad Coulter that morning."

I said, "Granddad?"

And then she told me the story. She told it quietly, looking through the window into that July morning in 1912. Her hands lay in her lap and never moved. The only effect her telling had on her was a glistening that appeared from time to time in her eyes. She told the story well, giving many details. She had a good memory, and she had lived many years with her mother-in-law, who also had a good one. I have the impression that they, but not my grandfather, had pondered together over the event many times. She spoke as if she were seeing it all happen, even the parts of it that she had in fact not seen.

"If it hadn't been for Jack Beechum, Mat *would* have killed him," my grandmother said.

That was the point. Or it was one of the points—the one, perhaps, that she most wanted me to see. But it was not the beginning of the story. Adam and Eve and then Cain and Abel began it, as my grandmother depended on me to know. Even in Thad Coulter's part of the story, the beginning was some years earlier than the July of 1912.

Abner Coulter, Thad's only son, had hired himself out

to a grocer in Hargrave. After a few years, when he had (in his own estimation) learned the trade, he undertook to go into business for himself in competition with his former employer. He rented a building right on the court-house square. He was enabled to do this by a sizable sum of money borrowed from the Hargrave bank on a note secured by a mortgage on his father's farm.

And here Thad's character enters into the story. For Thad not only secured his son's note with the farm that was all he had in the world and that he had only recently finished paying for but he further committed himself by bragging in Port William of his son's new status as a merchant in the county seat.

"Thad Coulter was not a bad man," my grandmother said. "I believed then, and I believe now, that he was not a bad man. But we are all as little children. Some know it and some don't."

She looked at me to see if I was one who knew it, and I nodded, but I was thirty then and did not know it yet.

"He was as a little child," she said, "and he was in serious trouble."

He had in effect given his life and its entire effort as hostage to the possibility that Abner, his only son, could be made a merchant in a better place than Port William.

Before two years were out, Abner repaid his father's confidence by converting many small private fritterings and derelictions into an undisguisable public failure and thereupon by riding off to somewhere unknown on the back of a bay gelding borrowed ostensibly for an over-night trip to Port William. And so Thad's fate was passed from the reckless care of his son to the small mercy of the law. Without more help than he could confidently expect, he was going to lose his farm. Even with help, he was going to have to pay for it again, and he was close to sixty years old.

As he rode home from his interview with the Hargrave banker, in which the writing on the wall had been made plain to him, he was gouging his heel urgently into his mule's flank. Since he had got up out of the chair in the banker's office, he had been full of a desire as compelling as thirst to get home, to get stopped, to get low to the ground, as if to prevent himself from falling off the world. For the country that he had known all his life and had depended on, at least in dry weather, to be solid and steady underfoot had suddenly risen under him like a wave.

Needing help as he did, he could not at first bring himself to ask for it. Instead, he spent most of two days propped against a post in his barn, drinking heavily and talking aloud to himself about betrayal, ruin, the cold-heartedness of the Hargrave bankers, and the poor doings of damned fools, meaning both Abner and himself. And he recalled, with shocks of bitterness that only the whiskey could assuage, his confident words in Port William about Abner and his prospects.

"I worked for it, and I come to own it," he said over and over again. "Now them will own it that never worked for it. And him that stood on it to mount up into the world done run to perdition without a patch, damn him, to cover his ass or a rag to hide his face."

When his wife and daughter begged him to come into the house, he said that a man without the sense to keep a house did not deserve to be in one. He said he would shelter with the dogs and hogs, where he belonged.

The logical source of help was Ben Feltner. Ben had helped Thad to buy his farm—had signed his note and stood behind him. Ben was his friend, and friendship mattered to Ben; it may have mattered to him above all. But Thad did not go to Ben until after his second night in the barn. He walked to Ben's house in Port William early in the morning, drunk and unsteady, his mind tattered and raw from repeated plunges through the thorns and briars of his ruin.

Ben was astonished by the look of him. Thad had always been a man who used himself hard, and he had grown gaunt and stooped, his mouth slowly caving in as he lost his teeth. But that morning he was also soiled, sagging, unshaved and uncombed, his eyes bloodshot and glary. But Ben said, "Come in, Thad. Come in and sit down." And he took him by the arm, led him in to a chair, and sat down facing him.

"They got me, Ben," Thad said, the flesh twitching around his eyes. "They done got me to where I can't get loose." His eyes glazed by tears that never fell, he made as much sense of his calamity as he was able to make: "A poor man don't stand no show." And then, his mind lurching on, unable to stop, he fell to cursing, first Abner, and then the Hargrave bank, and then the ways of the world that afforded no show to a poor man.

Ben listened to it all, sitting with his elbow on the chair arm and his forefinger pointed against his cheek. Thad's language and his ranting in that place would not have been excusable had he been sober. But insofar as

Thad was drunk, Ben was patient. He listened attentively, his eyes on Thad's face, except that from time to time he looked down at his beard as if to give Thad an opportunity to see that he should stop.

Finally Ben stopped him. "Thad, I'll tell you what. I don't believe I can talk with you anymore this morning. Go home, now, and get sober and come back. And then we'll see."

Thad did not have to take Ben's words as an insult. But in his circumstances and condition, it was perhaps inevitable that he would. That Ben was his friend made the offense worse—far worse. In refusing to talk to him as he was, Ben, it seemed to Thad, had exiled him from the society of human beings, had withdrawn the last vestige of a possibility that he might find anywhere a redemption for himself, much less for his forfeited land. For Thad was not able then to distinguish between himself as he was and himself as he might be sober. He saw himself already as a proven fool, fit only for the company of dogs and hogs. If he could have accepted this judgment of himself, then his story would at least have been different and would perhaps have been better. But while he felt the force and truth of his own judgment, he raged against it. He had fled to Ben, hoping that somehow, by some means that he could not imagine, Ben could release him from the solitary cage of his self-condemnation. And now Ben had shut the door.

Thad's whole face began to twitch and his hands to move aimlessly, as if his body were being manipulated from the inside by some intention that he could not control. Patches of white appeared under his whiskers. He said, "I cuss you to your damned face, Ben Feltner, for I have come to you with my hat in my hand and you have spit in it. You have throwed in your lot with them sons of bitches against me."

At that Ben reached his limit. Yet even then he did not become angry. He was a large, unfearful man, and his self-defense had something of merriment in it. He stood up. "Now, Thad, my friend," he said, "you must go." And he helped him to the door. He did not do so violently or with an excess of force. But though he was seventy-two years old, Ben was still in hearty strength, and he helped Thad to the door in such a way that Thad had no choice but to go.

But Thad did not go home. He stayed, hovering about the front of the house, for an hour or more.

"It seemed like hours and hours that he stayed out there," my grandmother said. She and my great-grandmother, Nancy, and old Aunt Cass, the cook, had overheard the conversation between Ben and Thad, or had overheard at least Thad's part of it, and afterward they watched him from the windows, for his fury had left an influence. The house was filled with a quiet that seemed to remember with sorrow the quiet that had been in it before Thad had come.

The morning was bright and still, and it was getting hot, but Thad seemed unable to distinguish between sun and shade. There had got to be something fluttery or mothlike about him now, so erratic and unsteady and unceasing were his movements. He was talking to himself, nodding or shaking his head, his hands making sudden strange motions without apparent reference to whatever he might have been saying. Now and again he started resolutely toward the house and then swerved away.

All the while the women watched. To my grandmother, remembering, it seemed that they were surrounded by signs that had not yet revealed their significance. Aunt Cass told her afterward, "I dreamed of the dark, Miss Margaret, all full of the sound of crying, and I knowed it was something bad." And it seemed to my grandmother, as she remembered, that she too had felt the house and town and the bright day itself all enclosed in that dreamed darkness full of the sounds of crying.

Finally, looking out to where the road from upriver came over the rise into town, they saw a team and wagon coming. Presently they recognized Thad Coulter's team, a pair of mare mules, one black and the other once gray but now faded to white. They were driven by Thad's daughter, wearing a sunbonnet, a sun-bleached blue cotton dress, and an apron.

"It's Martha Elizabeth," Nancy said.

And Aunt Cass said, "Poor child."

"Well," Nancy said, relieved, "she'll take him home."

When Martha Elizabeth came to where Thad was, she stopped the mules and got down. So far as they could see from the house, she did not plead with him. She did not say anything at all. She took hold of him, turned him toward the wagon, and led him to it. She held onto him as he climbed unsteadily up into the wagon and sat down on the spring seat, and then, gathering her skirts in one hand, she climbed up and sat beside him. And all the while she was gentle with him. Afterward and always, my grandmother remembered how gentle Martha Elizabeth had been with him.

Martha Elizabeth turned the team around, and the Feltner women watched the wagon with its troubled burden go slowly back along the ridgeline. When it had disappeared, they went back to their housework.

Ben, who had meant to go to the field where his hands were at work, did not leave the house as long as Thad was waiting about outside. He saw no point in antagonizing Thad when he did not have to, and so he sat down with a newspaper.

When he knew that Thad was gone and had had time to be out of sight, Ben got up and put on his hat and went out. He was worried about the state both of Thad's economy and of his mind. He thought he might find some of the other Coulters in town. He didn't know that he would, but it was Saturday, and he probably would.

The Feltner house stood, as it still does, in the overlap of the northeast corner of the town and the southwest corner of Ben's farm, which spread away from the house and farmstead over the ridges and hollows and down the side of the valley to the river. There was a farmstead at each of the town's four corners. There was, as there still is, only the one road, which climbed out of the river valley, crossed a mile of ridge, passed through the town, and, after staying on the ridge another half mile or so, went back down into the valley again. For most of its extent, at that time, it was little more than a wagon track. Most of the goods that reached the Port William merchants still came to the town landing by steamboat and then up the hill by team and wagon. The town itself consisted of perhaps two dozen houses, a church, a blacksmith shop, a bank, a barber shop, a doctor's office, a hotel, two saloons, and four stores that sold a variety of merchandise from groceries to dry goods to hardware to harness. The road that passed through town was there only as a casual and hardly foreseen result of the comings and goings of the inhabitants. An extemporaneous town government had from time to time caused a few loads of creek rock to be hauled and knapped and spread over it, and the townspeople had flung their ashes into it, but that was all. It had never thought of calling itself a street.

Though the houses and shops had been connected for some time by telephone lines carried overhead on peeled and whitewashed locust poles, there was as yet not an automobile in the town. There were times in any year still when Port William could not have been reached by an automobile that was not accompanied by a team of mules to pull it across the creeks and out of the mud holes.

Except for the telephone lines, the town, as it looked to Ben Feltner on that July morning seventy-eight years ago, might have been unchanged for many more years than it had existed. It looked older than its history. And yet in Port William, as everywhere else, it was already the second decade of the twentieth century. And in some of the people of the town and the community surrounding

it, one of the characteristic diseases of the twentieth century was making its way: the suspicion that they would
be greatly improved if they were someplace else. This
disease had entered into Thad Coulter and into Abner.
In Thad it was fast coming to crisis. If Port William could
not save him, then surely there was another place that
could. But Thad could not just leave, as Abner had; Port
William had been too much his life for that. And he was
held also by friendship—by his friendship for Ben Feltner, and for himself as a man whom Ben Feltner had
befriended—a friendship that Ben Feltner seemed now
to have repudiated and made hateful. Port William was
a stumbling block to Thad, and he must rid himself of it
somehow.

Ben, innocent of the disease that afflicted his friend
yet mortally implicated in it and not knowing it, made
his way down into the town, looking about in order to
gauge its mood—for Port William had its moods, and
they needed watching. More energy was generated in the
community than the work of the community could consume, and the surplus energy often went into fighting.
There had been cuttings and shootings enough. But usually the fighting was more primitive, and the combatants
simply threw whatever projectiles came to hand: corncobs, snowballs, green walnuts, or rocks. In the previous
winter, a young Coulter by the name of Burley had
claimed that he had had an eye blackened by a frozen
horse turd thrown, so far as he could determine, by a
Power of the Air. But the place that morning was quiet.
Most of the crops had been laid by and many of the
farmers were already in town, feeling at ease and inclined

to rest now that their annual battle with the weeds had ended. They were sitting on benches and kegs or squatting on their heels under the shade trees in front of the stores, or standing in pairs or small groups among the hitched horses along the sides of the road. Ben passed among them, greeting them and pausing to talk, enjoying himself, and all the while on the lookout for one or another of the Coulters.

Martha Elizabeth was Thad's youngest, the last at home. She had, he thought, the levelest head of any of his children and was the best. Assuming the authority that his partiality granted her, she had at fifteen taken charge of the household, supplanting her mother, who was sickly, and her three older sisters, who had married and gone. At seventeen, she was responsible beyond her years. She was a tall, raw-boned girl, with large hands and feet, a red complexion, and hair so red that, in the sun, it appeared to be on fire.

"Everybody loved Martha Elizabeth," my grandmother said. "She was as good as ever was."

To Thad it was a relief to obey her, to climb into the wagon under the pressure of her hand on his arm and to sit beside her as she drove the team homeward through the rising heat of the morning. Her concern for him gave him shelter. Holding to the back of the seat, he kept himself upright and, for the moment, rested in being with her.

But when they turned off the ridge onto the narrower road that led down into the valley called Cattle Pen and came in sight of their place, she could no longer shelter him. It had long been, to Thad's eye, a pretty farm—a hundred or so acres of slope and ridge on the west side of the little valley, the lower, gentler slopes divided from the ridge land by a ledgy bluff that was wooded, the log house and other buildings occupying a shelf above the creek bottom. Through all his years of paying for it, he had aspired toward it as toward a Promised Land. To have it, he had worked hard and long and deprived himself, and Rachel, his wife, had deprived herself. He had worked alone more often than not. Abner, as he grew able, had helped, as the girls had, also. But Abner had been reserved for something better. Abner was smart—too smart, as Thad and Rachel agreed, without ever much talking about it, to spend his life farming a hillside. Something would have to be done to start him on his way to something better, a Promised Land yet more distant.

Although he had thought the farm not good enough for Abner, Thad was divided in his mind; for himself he loved it. It was what he had transformed his life into. And now, even in the morning light, it lay under the shadow of his failure, and he could not bear to look at it. It was his life, and he was no longer in it. Somebody else, some other thing that did not even know it, stood ready to take possession of it. He was ashamed in its presence. To look directly at it would be like looking Martha Elizabeth full in the eyes, which he could not do either. And his shame raged in him.

When she stopped in the lot in front of the barn and helped him down, he started unhitching the team. But she took hold of his arm and drew him away gently toward the house.

"Come on, now," she said. "You've got to have you something to eat and some rest."

But he jerked away from her. "Go see to your mammy!"

"No," she said. "Come on." And she attempted again to move him toward the house.

He pushed her away, and she fell. He could have cut off his hand for so misusing her, and yet his rage at himself included her. He reached into the wagon box and took out a short hickory stock with a braid of rawhide knotted to it. He shook it at her.

"Get up," he said. "Get yonder to that house 'fore I wear you out."

He had never spoken to her in such a way, had never imagined himself doing so. He hated what he had done, and he could not undo it.

The heat of the day had established itself now. There was not a breeze anywhere, not a breath. A still haze filled the valley and redoubled the light. Within that blinding glare he occupied a darkness that was loud with accusing cries.

Martha Elizabeth stood at the kitchen door a moment, looking back at him, and then she went inside. Thad turned back to the team then, unhitched them, did up the lines, and led the mules to their stalls in the barn. He moved as if dreaming through these familiar motions that had now estranged themselves from him. The closer he had come to home, the more the force of his failure had gathered there to exclude him.

And it was Ben Feltner who had barred the door and left him without a friend. Ben Feltner, who owed nothing, had turned his back on his friend, who now owed everything.

He said aloud, "Yes, I'll come back sober, God damn you to Hell!"

He lifted the jug out of the white mule's manger, pulled the cob from its mouth, and drank. When he lowered it, it was empty. It had lasted him three days, and now it was empty. He cocked his wrist and broke the jug against an upright.

"Well, that does for you, old holler-head."

He stood, letting the whiskey seek its level in him, and felt himself slowly come into purpose; now he had his anger full and clear. Now he was summoned by an almost visible joy.

He went to the house, drank from the water bucket on the back porch, and stepped through the kitchen door. Rachel and Martha Elizabeth were standing together by the cookstove, facing him.

"Thad, honey, I done fixed dinner," Rachel said. "Set down and eat."

He opened the stairway door, stepped up, and took down his pistol from the little shelf over the door frame.

"No, now," Martha Elizabeth said. "Put that away. You ain't got a use in this world for that."

"Don't contrary me," Thad said. "Don't you say another damned word."

He put the pistol in his hip pocket with the barrel sticking up and turned to the door.

"Wait, Thad," Rachel said. "Eat a little before you

go." But she was already so far behind him that he hardly heard her.

He walked to the barn, steadying himself by every upright thing he came to, so that he proceeded by a series of handholds on doorjamb and porch post and gatepost and tree. He could no longer see the place but walked in a shifting aisle of blinding light through a cloud of darkness. Behind him now was almost nothing. And ahead of him was the singular joy to which his heart now beat in answer.

He went into the white mule's stall, unbuckled hame strap and bellyband, and shoved the harness off her back, letting it fall. He unbuckled the collar and let it fall. Again his rage swelled within him, seeming to tighten the skin of his throat, as though his body might fail to contain it, for he had never before in his life allowed a mule's harness to touch the ground if he could help it. But he was not in his life now, and his rage pleased him.

He hooked his finger in the bit ring and led the mule to the drinking trough by the well in front of the barn. The trough was half an oak barrel, nearly full of water. The mule wanted to drink, but he jerked her head up and drew her forward until she stood beside the trough. The shorn stubble of her mane under his hand, he stepped up onto the rim. Springing, he cast himself across the mule's back, straddled her, and sat upright as darkness swung around him. He jerked hard at the left rein.

"Get up, Beck," he said.

The mule was as principled as a martyr. She would have died before she would have trotted a step, and yet he urged her forward with his heel. Even as the hind feet of the mule lifted from their tracks, the thought of Martha Elizabeth formed itself within the world's ruin. She seemed to rise up out of its shambles, like a ghost or an influence. She would follow him. He needed to hurry.

On the fringe of the Saturday bustle in front of the business houses, Ben met Early Rowanberry and his little boy, Arthur. Early was carrying a big sack, and Art a small one. They had started out not long after breakfast; from the log house on the ridgetop where the Rowanberrys had settled before Kentucky was a state, they had gone down the hill, forded the creek known as Sand Ripple, and then walked up the Shade Branch hollow through the Feltner Place and on to town. Early had done his buying and a little talking, had bought a penny's worth of candy for Art, and now they were starting the long walk back. Ben knew that they had made the trip on foot to spare their mules, though the sacks would weigh sorely on their shoulders before they made it home.

"Well, Early," Ben said, "you've got a good hand with you today, I see."

"He's tol'ble good company, Ben, and he packs a little load," Early said.

Ben liked all the Rowanberrys, who had been good neighbors to him all his life, and Early was a better-than-average Rowanberry—a quiet man with a steady gaze and a sort of local fame for his endurance at hard work.

Ben then offered his hand to Art, who shyly held out his own. But then Ben said, "My boy, are you going to grow up to be a wheelhorse like your pap?" and Art answered without hesitation, "Yes, sir."

"Ah, that's right," Ben said. And he placed his hand on the boy's unladen shoulder.

The two Rowanberrys then resumed their homeward journey, and Ben walked on down the edge of the dusty road into town.

Ben was in no hurry. He had his mission in mind and was somewhat anxious about it, but he gave it its due place in the order of things. Thad's difficulty was not simple; whatever it was possible to do for him could not be done in a hurry. Ben passed slowly through the talk of the place and time, partaking of it. He liked the way the neighborhood gathered into itself on such days. Now and then, in the midst of the more casual conversation, a little trade talk would rouse up over a milk cow or a pocketknife or a saddle or a horse or mule. Or there would be a joke or a story or a bit of news, uprisings of the town's interest in itself that would pass through it and die away like scurries of wind. It was close to noon. It was hot even in the shade now, and the smells of horse sweat and horse manure had grown strong. On the benches and kegs along the storefronts, pocketknives were busy. Profound meditations were coming to bear upon long scrolls of cedar or poplar curling backward over thumbs and wrists and piling over shoetops.

Somebody said, "Well, I can see the heat waves a-rising."

Somebody else said, "Ain't nobody but a lazy man can see them heat waves."

And then Ben saw Thad's cousin, Dave Coulter, and Dave's son, Burley, coming out of one of the stores, Dave with a sack of flour on his shoulder and Burley with a sack of meal on his. Except for his boy's face and grin, Burley was a grown man. He was seventeen, a square-handed, muscular fellow already known for the funny things he said, though his elders knew of them only by hearsay. He and his father turned down the street toward their wagon, and Ben followed them.

When they had hunched the sacks off their shoulders into the wagon, Ben said, "Dave?"

Dave turned to him and stuck out his hand. "Why, howdy, Ben."

"How are you, Dave?"

" 'Bout all right, I reckon."

"And how are you, Burley?"

Dave turned to his boy to see that he would answer properly; Burley, grinning, said, "Doing about all right, thank you, sir," and Dave turned back to Ben.

"Had to lay in a little belly timber," he said, " 'gainst we run plumb out. And the boy here, he wanted to come see the sights."

"Well, my boy," Ben said, "have you learned anything worthwhile?"

Burley grinned again, gave a quick nod, and said, "Yessir."

"Oh, hit's an educational place," Dave said. "We hung into one of them educational conversations yonder in the store. That's why we ain't hardly going to make it back home by dinnertime."

"Well, I won't hold you up for long," Ben said. And

he told Dave as much as he had understood of Thad's trouble. They were leaning against the wagon box, facing away from the road. Burley, who had gone to untie the mules, was still standing at their heads.

"Well," Dave said, "hit's been norated around that Abner weren't doing just the way he ought to. Tell you the truth, I been juberous about that loan proposition ever since Thad put his name to it. Put his whole damned foothold in that damned boy's pocket is what he done. And now you say it's all gone up the spout."

"He's in a serious fix, no question about it."

"Well, is there anything a feller can do for him?"

"Well, there's one thing for certain. He was drunk when he came to see me. He was cussing and raring. If you, or some of you, could get him sober, it would help. And then we could see if we can help him out of his scrape."

"Talking rough, was he?"

"Rough enough."

"I'm sorry, Ben. Thad don't often drink, but when he does he drinks like the Lord appointed him to get rid of it all."

Somebody said, "Look out!"

They turned to see Thad and the white mule almost abreast of them. Thad was holding the pistol.

"They said he just looked awful," my grandmother said. "He looked like death warmed over."

Ben said, without raising his voice, in the same reasonable tone in which he had been speaking to Dave, "Hold on, Thad."

And Thad fired.

Dave saw a small round red spot appear in the center of Ben's forehead. A perplexed look came to his face, as if he had been intending to say something more and had forgot what it was. For a moment, he remained standing just as he had been, one hand on the rim of the wagon box. And then he fell. As he went down, his shoulder struck the hub of the wagon wheel so that he fell onto his side, his hat rolling underneath the wagon.

Thad put the pistol back into his pocket. The mule had stood as still after he had halted her as if she were not there at all but at home under a tree in the pasture. When Thad kicked her, she went on again.

Ben Feltner never had believed in working on Sunday, and he did not believe in not working on workdays. Those two principles had shaped all his weeks. He liked to make his hay cuttings and begin other large, urgent jobs as early in the week as possible in order to have them finished before Sunday. On Saturdays, he and Mat and the hands worked in the crops if necessary; otherwise, that day was given to the small jobs of maintenance that the farm constantly required and to preparations for Sunday, when they would do nothing except milk and feed. When the work was caught up and the farm in order, Ben liked to have everybody quit early on Saturday afternoon. He liked the quiet that descended over the place then, with the day of rest ahead.

On that Saturday morning he had sent Old Smoke, Aunt Cass's husband, and their son, Samp, and Samp's boy, Joe, to mend a fence back on the river bluff. Mat he sent to the blacksmith shop to have the shoes reset on Governor, his buggy horse. They would not need Governor to go to church; they walked to church. But when they had no company on Sunday afternoon and the day was fair, Ben and Nancy liked to drive around the neighborhood, looking at the crops and stopping at various households to visit. They liked especially to visit Nancy's brother, Jack Beechum, and his wife, Ruth, who lived on the Beechum home place, the place that Nancy would always refer to as "out home."

And so Mat that morning, after his chores were done, had slipped a halter on Governor and led him down through town to the blacksmith's. He had to wait—there were several horses and mules already in line—and so he tied Governor to the hitch rail in front of the shop and went in among the others who were waiting and talking, figuring that he would be late for dinner.

It was a good place. The shop stood well back from the street, leaving in front of it a tree-shaded, cinder-covered yard, which made room for the hitch rail and for the wagons, sleds, and other implements waiting to be repaired. The shop itself was a single large, dirt-floored room, meticulously clean—every surface swept and every tool in place. Workbenches went around three walls. Near the large open doorway were the forge and anvil.

The blacksmith—a low, broad, grizzled man by the name of Elder Johnson—was the best within many miles, a fact well known to himself, which sometimes made him difficult. He also remembered precisely every horse or mule he had ever nailed a shoe on, and so he was one of the keepers of the town's memory.

Elder was shoeing a colt that was nervous and was giving him trouble. He was working fast so as to cause the colt as little discomfort as he could. He picked up the left hind hoof, caught it between his aproned knees, and laid the shoe on it. The shoe was too wide at the heel, and he let the colt's foot go back to the floor. A small sharp-faced man smoking a cob pipe was waiting, holding out a broken singletree for Elder's inspection as he passed on his way back to the forge.

Elder looked as if the broken tree were not the sort of thing that could concern him.

"Could I get this done by this evening?" the man asked. His name was Skeets Willard, and his work was always in some state of emergency. "I can't turn a wheel," he said, "till I get that fixed."

Elder let fall the merest glance at the two pieces of the singletree, and then looked point-blank at the man himself as if surprised not only by his presence but by his existence. "What the hell do you think I am? A hammer with a brain? Do you see all them horses and mules tied up out there? If you want that fixed, I'll fix it when I can. If you don't, take it home."

Skeets Willard elected to lay the pieces down in a conspicuous place by the forge. And Elder, whose outburst had not interrupted the flow of talk among the bystanders, caught the shoe in his tongs and shoved it in among the coals of the forge. He cranked the bellows and made small flames spike up out of the coals. As he turned the handle, he stared in a kind of trance at the light of the open doorway, and the light shone in his eyes, and his face and his arms were shining with sweat. Presently he drew the shoe, glowing, out of the coals and, laying it on the horn of the anvil, turned in the heel. He then plunged the shoe into the slack tub from which it raised a brief shriek of steam.

Somebody turned out of the conversation and said, "Say, Elder, do you remember that little red mule come in here with a bunch of yearlings Marce Catlett bought up around Lexington? Ned, I think they called him."

"Newt," Elder said in so even a voice that Skeets Willard might never have been there. "You bet I remember him."

He took the cooled shoe from the slack tub and, picking up the colt's foot and straddling it again, quickly nailed one nail in each side, raking the points over with the claws of his hammer. He let the colt stand on his foot again to see how the shoe set. "You bet I remember him," he said. "That mule could kick the lard out of a biscuit."

And then they heard the single voice raised in warning out in the road, followed immediately by the shot and by a rising murmur of excited, indistinguishable voices as the whole Saturday crowd turned its attention to the one thing.

Mat hurried out with the others and saw the crowd wedged in between the storefronts and Dave Coulter's wagon. He only began to realize that the occasion concerned him when the crowd began to make way for him as he approached.

"Let him through! Let him through!" the crowd said.

The crowd opened to let him through, turning its faces to him, falling silent as it saw who he was. And then he saw what was left of the man who had been his father lying against the wagon wheel. Those nearest him heard him say, "Oh!" and it did not sound like him at all. He stepped forward and knelt and took his father's wrist in his hand to feel for the pulse that he did not expect, having seen the wound and the fixed unsighted eyes. The crowd now was as quiet around him as the still treetops along the road. For what seemed a long time Mat knelt there with his father's dead wrist in his hand, while his mind arrived and arrived and yet arrived at that place and time and that body lying still on the soiled and blood-ied stones. When he looked up again, he did not look like the man they had known at all.

"Who did this?" he said.

And the crowd answered, "Thad Coulter, he done it."

"Where'd he go?"

"He taken down the road yonder towards Hargrave. He was on that old white mule, old May."

When Mat stood up again from his father's side, he was a man new-created by rage. All that he had been and thought and done gave way to his one desire to kill the man who had killed his father. He ached, mind and body, with the elation of that one thought. He was not armed, but he never thought of that. He would go for the horse he had left tied at the blacksmith's. He would ride Thad Coulter down. He would come up beside him and club him off the mule. He would beat him down out of the air. And in that thought, which lived more in his right arm than in his head, both he and his enemy were as clear of history as if newborn.

By the time Mat was free of the crowd, he was running.

Jack Beechum had sold a team of mules the day before, and so he had a check to carry to the bank. He also had a list of things that Ruth wanted from town, and now that he had money ahead he wanted to settle his account at Chatham's store. His plan was to do his errands in town and get back home by dinner; that afternoon, he wanted to mow a field of hay, hoping it would cure by Monday. He rode to town on a good black gelding, called Socks for his four white pasterns.

He tied the horse some distance from the center of town in a place of better shade and fewer flies. He went to the bank first and then went about gathering the things that Ruth needed, ending up at Chatham's. He was sitting by Beater Chatham's desk in the back, watching Beater total up his account, when they heard the shot out in the street.

"Sounds like they're getting Saturday started out there," Jack said.

"I reckon," Beater said, checking his figures.

"They're going to keep on until they shoot somebody who don't deserve it."

Beater looked at him then over the tops of his glasses. "Well, they'll have to look around outside town to find somebody, won't they?" He filled out a check for the amount of the bill and handed the check to Jack for him to sign.

And then someone who had just stepped out of the store stepped back in again and said, "Jack, you'd better come. They've shot Ben Feltner."

Jack never signed the check that day or for several days. He ran to the door. When he was outside, he saw first the crowd and then Mat running toward him out of it. Without breaking his own stride, he caught Mat and held him.

They were both moving at some speed, and the crowd heard the shock of the impact as the two men came together. Jack could hardly have known what he was doing. He had had no time to think. He may have been moved by an impulse simply to stop things until he *could* think. Or perhaps he knew by the look on Mat's face that he had to be obstructed. At any rate, as soon as Jack had taken hold of Mat, he understood that he *had* to hold him. And he knew that he had never taken hold of any such thing before. He had caught Mat in a sideways hug that clamped his arms to his sides. Jack's sole task was to keep Mat from freeing his arms. But Mat was little more than half Jack's age; he was in the prime of his strength. And now he twisted and strained with the concentration of fury, uttering cries that could have been either grunts or sobs, forcing Jack both to hold him and to hold him up. They strove there a long time, heaving and staggering, hardly moving from the tracks they had stood in when they came together, and the dust rose up around them. Jack felt that his arms would pull apart at the joints. He ached afterward. Something went out of him that day, and he was not the same again.

And what went out of Jack came into Mat. Or so it

seemed, for in that desperate embrace he became a stronger man than he had been. A strength came into him that held his grief and his anger as Jack had held him. And Jack knew of the coming of this strength, not because it enabled Mat to break free but because it enabled Jack to turn him loose. Mat ceased to strive, and Jack let go his hold. He stepped away, allowing himself to be recognized, and Mat stood. To Jack, it was as though he had caught one man and let another go.

But he put his eye on Mat, not willing yet to trust him entirely to himself, and waited.

They both were winded, wet with sweat, and for a moment they only breathed, watched by the crowd, Jack watching Mat, Mat looking at nothing.

As they stood so, the girl, Martha Elizabeth, walked by in the road. She did not look at them or at the wagon or at the body crumpled on the ground. She walked past it all, looking ahead, as if she already saw what she was walking toward.

Coming aware that Jack was waiting on him, Mat looked up; he met Jack's gaze. He said, "Pa's dead. Thad Coulter has shot him."

They waited, looking at each other still, while the earth shook under them.

Mat said, "I'll go tell Ma. You bring Pa, but give me a little time."

Dinner was ready, and the men were late.

"It wasn't usual for them to be late," my grandmother said, "but we didn't think yet that anything was wrong.

Your mother was just a little girl then, and she was telling us a story about a doll and a dog and a horse."

Aunt Cass stood by the stove, keeping an eye on the griddle. Nancy was sweeping the floor under the firebox of the stove; she was a woman who was always doing. Margaret, having set the table, had turned one of the chairs out into the floor and sat down. All three were listening to Bess, who presently stopped her story, rolled her eyes, and said, "I hear my innards a-growling. I reckon I must be hungry."

They laughed.

"I spect so, I spect so," Aunt Cass said. "Well, you'll get something to eat fore long."

When she heard Mat at the kitchen door, Aunt Cass said, "Miss Nancy, you want to take the hoecake up?" And then seeing the change in Mat's face, which was new to it but old to the world, she hushed and stood still. Nancy, seeing the expression on Cass's face, turned to look at Mat.

Bess said, "Goody! Now we can eat!"

Mat looked at his mother and then down at Bess and smiled. "You can eat directly," he said.

And then he said, "Margaret, take Bess and go upstairs. I think she's got a book up there she wants you to read to her."

"I knew what it was then," my grandmother said. "Oh, I felt it go all over me before I knew it in my mind. I just wanted to crawl away. But I had your mother to think about. You always have somebody to think about, and it's a blessing."

She said, "Come on, Bess, let's go read a story. We'll eat in a little bit."

As soon as he heard their footsteps going up the stairs, Mat looked at his mother again. As the silence gathered against him, he said, "Ma, I'm sorry, Pa's dead. Thad Coulter has shot him."

She was already wearing black. She had borne four children and raised one. Two of her children she had buried in the same week of a diphtheria epidemic, of which she had nearly died herself. After the third child had died, she never wore colors again. It was not that she chose to be ostentatiously bereaved. She could not have chosen to be ostentatious about anything. She was, in fact, a woman possessed of a strong native cheerfulness. And yet she had accepted a certain darkness that she had lived in too intimately to deny.

She stood, looking at Mat, while she steadied herself and steadied the room around her, in the quiet that, having suddenly begun there, would not end for a long time. And then she said to Mat, "Sit down."

She said, "Cass, sit down."

They turned chairs away from the table and sat down, and then she did.

"Now," she said, "I want to know what happened."

In the quiet Mat told as much, as little, as he knew.

As if to exert herself against the silence that too quickly filled the room, Nancy stood again. She laid her hand on the shoulder of Mat's wet shirt and patted it once.

"Cass," she said, "we mustn't cry," though there were tears on her own face.

"Mat," she said, "go get Smoke and Samp and Joe. Tell them, and tell them to come here."

To Aunt Cass again, she said, "We must fix the bed. They'll need a place to lay him."

And then they heard the burdened footsteps at the door.

In his cresting anger in the minutes before he stopped the mule in the road in Port William and fired the one shot that he ever fired in anger in his life, Thad Coulter knew a fierce, fulfilling joy. He saw the shot home to the mark, saw Ben Feltner stand a moment and go down, and then he heeled the mule hard in the side and rode on. He went on because all behind him that he might once have turned back to was gone from his mind, and perhaps even in his joy he knew that from that time there was to be no going back.

Even before the town was out of sight behind him, his anger and his joy began to leave him. It was as if his life's blood were running out of him, and he tried to stanch the flow by muttering aloud the curses of his rage. But they had no force, and his depletion continued.

His first thought beyond his anger was of the mule. She was thirsty, he knew, and he had denied her a drink.

"When we get to the creek," he said.

The mule followed the windings of the road down off the upland. Below the cleared ridges, they passed through woods. On the gentler open slopes below, they came into the blank sunlight again, and he could see the river winding between its wooded banks toward its meeting with the Ohio at Hargrave.

At the foot of the hill, the road dipped under trees again and forded a creek. Thad rode the mule into the pool above the ford, loosened the rein, and let her drink. It was a quiet, deeply shaded place, the water unrippled until the mule stepped into it. For the first time in three days Thad could hear the quiet, and a bottomless sorrow opened in him, causing him suddenly to clutch his belly and groan aloud.

When the mule had finished drinking, he rode her out of the pool, dismounted, and, unbuckling one end of the rein from the bit, led her into a clump of bushes and tall weeds and tied her there. For now the thought of pursuit had come to him, and he knew he would have to go the rest of the way on foot. The mule could not be hurried, and she would be difficult to hide.

He went back to the pool and knelt at the edge of it and drank, and then he washed his hands and in his cupped hands lifted the clear water time and again to his face.

Presently, he became still, listening. He could hear nothing but the cicadas in the surrounding trees. And then he heard, coming fast, the sound of loud talking and the rapid hooftread of horses. He stepped into a patch of weeds and watched several riders go by on the road. They were boys and young men from the town who, having waited through the aftermath of the shooting, had now been carried by their excitement into pursuit of him. "Boys," he thought. He felt in no danger from them—

he did not think of the pistol—and yet he feared them. He imagined himself hurrying on foot along the road, while the young riders picked and pecked at him.

The quiet returned, and he could feel, as if in the hair roots and pores of his skin, that Martha Elizabeth was coming near. He went back to the road again.

The walking and the water drying on his face cleared his mind, and now he knew himself as he had been and as he was and knew that he was changed beyond unchanging into something he did not love. Now that his anger had drained away, his body seemed to him not only to be a burden almost too heavy to carry but to be on the verge of caving in. He walked with one hand pressed to his belly where the collapse seemed already to have begun.

The best way between Port William and Hargrave was still the river. The road found its way as if by guess, bent this way and that by the whims of topography and the convenience of landowners. At intervals, it was interrupted by farm gates.

After a while, hearing several more horses coming behind him, he stepped out of the road and lay down in a small canebrake. When they had passed, he returned to the road and went on. Always he was watchful of the houses he passed, but he stayed in the road. If he was to protect the one choice of which he was still master, he had to hurry.

And now, as he had not been able to do when he left it, he could see his farm. It shone in his mind as if inwardly lighted in the darkness that now surrounded both him and it. He could see it with the morning sun dew-bright

on the woods and the sloping pastures, on the little crop-
lands on the ridge and in the bottoms along the creek.
He could see its cool shadows stretching out in the evening and the milk cows coming down the path to the
barn. It was irrevocably behind him now, as if a great
sword had fallen between him and it.

He was slow and small on the long road. The sun was
slow overhead. The air was heavy and unmoving. He
watched the steady stepping of his feet, the road going
backward beneath them. He had to get out of the road
only twice again: once for a family in a spring wagon
coming up from Hargrave and once for another horse
and rider coming down from Port William. Except for
those, nothing moved in the still heat but himself. Except
for the cicadas, the only sounds he heard were his own
steady footfalls on the dry dust.

He seemed to see always not only the changing road
beneath his feet but also that other world in which he
had lived, now lighted in the dark behind him, and it
came to him that on that day two lives had ended for a
possibility that never had existed: for Abner Coulter's
mounting up in a better place. And he felt the emptiness
open wider in him and again heard himself groan. He
wondered, so great was the pain of that emptiness, that
he did not weep, but it exceeded weeping as it exceeded
words. Beyond the scope of one man's grief, it cried out
in the air around him, as if in that day's hot light the
trees and the fields and the dust of the road all grieved.
An inward pressure that had given his body its shape
seemed to have been withdrawn, and he walked, holding himself, resisting step by step the urge to bend

around the emptiness opening in his middle and let himself fall.

Where the valley began to widen toward the river's mouth, the road passed a large bottom planted in corn. Thad looked back, expecting that he would see Martha Elizabeth, and he did see her. She was maybe three-quarters of a mile behind him, small in the distance, and the heat rising off the field shimmered and shook between them, but he knew her. He walked faster, and he did not look back again. It seemed to him that she knew everything he knew, and loved him anyhow. She loved him, minute by minute, not only as he had been but as he had become. It was a wonderful and a fearful thing to him that he had caused such a love for himself to come into the world and then had failed it. He could not have bowed low enough before it and remained above ground. He could not bear to think of it. But he knew that she walked behind him—balanced across the distance, in the same hot light, the same darkness, the same crying air—ever at the same speed that he walked.

Finally he came to the cluster of houses at Ellville, at the end of the bridge, and went across into Hargrave. From the bridge to the courthouse, he went ever deeper into the Saturday crowd, but he did not alter his gait or look at anybody. If anybody looked at him, he did not know it. At the cross streets, he could see on the river a towboat pushing a line of barges slowly upstream, black smoke gushing from its stacks. The walks were full of people, and the streets were full of buggies and wagons. He crossed the courthouse yard where people sat on benches or stood talking in little groups under the shade trees. It seemed to him that he walked in a world from which he had departed.

When he went through the front door of the courthouse into the sudden cool darkness of the hallway, he could not see. Lights swam in his eyes in the dark, and he had to prop himself against the wall. The place smelled of old paper and tobacco and of human beings, washed and unwashed. When he could see again, he walked to a door under a sign that said "Sheriff" and went in. It was a tall room lighted by two tall windows. There was a row of chairs for people to wait in, and several spittoons, placed at the presumed convenience of spitters, that had been as much missed as hit. No one was there but a large man in a broad-brimmed straw hat and a suit somewhat too small, who was standing behind a high desk, writing something. At first he did not look up. When he finally did look up, he stared at Thad for some time, as if not sufficiently convinced of what he saw.

"In a minute," he said, and looked down again and finished what he was writing. There was a badge pinned lopsidedly to the pocket of his shirt, and he held an unlit cigar like another pen in his left hand. He said as he wrote, "You been drove hard and put up wet, I reckon."

"Yes," Thad said. "I have killed a man."

The sheriff laid the pen on the blotter and looked up. "Who?"

Thad said, "Ben Feltner, the best friend I ever had." His eyes suddenly brimmed with tears, but they did not fall. He made no sound and he did not move.

"You're a Coulter, ain't you? From up about Port William?"

"Thad," Thad said.

The sheriff would have preferred that Thad had remained a fugitive. He did not want a self-confessed murderer on his hands—especially not one fresh from a Saturday killing in Port William. He knew Ben Feltner, knew he was liked, and feared there would be a commotion. Port William, as far as he was concerned, was nothing but trouble, almost beyond the law's reach and certainly beyond its convenience—a source, as far as he was concerned, of never foreseeable bad news. He did not know what would come next, but he thought that something would, and he did not approve of it.

"I wish to hell," he said, "that everybody up there who is going to kill each other would just by God go ahead and do it." He looked at Thad for some time in silence, as if giving him an opportunity to disappear.

"Well," he said, finally, "I reckon you just as well give me the pistol."

He gestured toward Thad's sagging hip pocket, and Thad took out the pistol and gave it to him.

"Come on," the sheriff said.

Thad followed him out a rear door into the small paved yard of the jail, where the sheriff rang for the jailer.

The sheriff had hardly got back into the office and taken up his work again when a motion in the doorway alerted him. He looked up and saw a big red-faced girl standing just outside the door as if uncertain whether or not it was lawful to enter. She wore a sunbonnet, a faded blue dress that reached to her ankles, and an apron. Though

46

she was obviously timid and unused to public places, she
returned his look with perfect candor.

"Come in," he said.

She crossed the threshold and again stopped.

"What can I do for you, miss?"

"I'm a-looking for Mr. Thad Coulter from up to Port
William, please, sir."

"You his daughter?"

"Yes, sir."

"Well, he's here. I got him locked up. He claims he
killed a fellow."

"He did," the girl said. "Is it allowed to see him?"

"Not now," the sheriff said. "You come back in the
morning, miss. You can see him then."

She stood looking at him another moment, as if to
make sure that he had said what he meant, and then she
said, "Well, I thank you," and went out.

An hour or so later, when he shut the office and started
home to supper, she was sitting on the end of one of the
benches under the shade trees, looking down at her hands
in her lap.

"You see," my grandmother said, "there are two deaths
in this—Mr. Feltner's and Thad Coulter's. We know Mr.
Feltner's because we had to know it. It was ours. That
we know Thad's is because of Martha Elizabeth. The
Martha Elizabeth you know."

I knew her, but it came strange to me now to think
of her—to be asked to see her—as a girl. She was what
I considered an old woman when I first remember her;

she was perhaps eight or ten years younger than my grandmother, the fire red long gone from her hair. She was a woman always near to smiling, sometimes to laughter. Her face, it seemed, had been made to smile. It was a face that assented wholly to the being of whatever and whomever she looked at. She had gone with her father to the world's edge and had come back with this smile on her face. Miss Martha Elizabeth, we younger ones called her. Everybody loved her.

When the sheriff came back from supper, she was still there on the bench, the Saturday night shoppers and talkers, standers and passers leaving a kind of island around her, as if unwilling to acknowledge the absolute submission they sensed in her. The sheriff knew as soon as he laid eyes on her this time that she was not going to go away. Perhaps he understood that she had no place to go that she could get to before it would be time to come back.

"Come on with me," he said, and he did not sound like a sheriff now but only a man.

She got up and followed him through the hallway of the courthouse, past the locked doors of the offices, out again, and across the little iron-fenced courtyard in front of the jail. The sheriff unlocked a heavy sheet-iron door, opened it, and closed it behind them, and they were in a large room of stone, steel, and concrete, containing several cages, barred from floor to ceiling, the whole interior lighted by one kerosene lamp hanging in the corridor.

Among the bars gleaming dimly and the shadows of bars thrown back against concrete and stone, she saw her father sitting on the edge of a bunk that was only an iron shelf let down on chains from the wall, with a thin mattress laid on it. He had paid no attention when they entered. He sat still, staring at the wall, one hand pressed against his belly, the other holding to one of the chains that supported the bunk.

The sheriff opened the cell door and stood aside to let her in. "I'll come back after while," he said.

The door closed and was locked behind her, and she stood still until Thad felt her presence and looked up. When he recognized her, he covered his face with both hands.

"He put his hands over his face like a man ashamed," my grandmother said. "But he was like a man, too, who had seen what he couldn't bear."

She sat without speaking a moment, looking at me, for she had much to ask of me.

"Maybe Thad saw his guilt full and clear then. But what he saw that he couldn't bear was something else."

And again she paused, looking at me. We sat facing each other on either side of the window; my grandfather lay in one of his lengthening sleeps nearby. The old house in that moment seemed filled with a quiet that extended not only out into the whole broad morning but endlessly both ways in time.

"People sometimes talk of God's love as if it's a pleasant thing. But it is terrible, in a way. Think of all it includes. It included Thad Coulter, drunk and mean and foolish, before he killed Mr. Feltner, and it included him afterwards."

She reached out then and touched the back of my right hand with her fingers; my hand still bears that touch, invisible and yet indelible as a tattoo.

"That's what Thad saw. He saw his guilt. He had killed his friend. He had done what he couldn't undo; he had destroyed what he couldn't make. But in the same moment he saw his guilt included in love that stood as near him as Martha Elizabeth and at that moment wore her flesh. It was surely weak and wrong of him to kill himself—to sit in judgment that way over himself. But surely God's love includes people who can't bear it."

The sheriff took Martha Elizabeth home with him that night; his wife fed her and turned back the bed for her in the spare room. The next day she sat with her father in his cell.

"All that day," my grandmother said, "he would hardly take his hands from his face. Martha Elizabeth fed him what little he would eat and raised the cup to his lips for what little he would drink. And he ate and drank only because she asked him to, almost not at all. I don't know what they said. Maybe nothing."

At bedtime again that night Martha Elizabeth went home with the sheriff. When they returned to the courthouse on Monday morning, Thad Coulter was dead by his own hand.

"It's a hard story to have to know," my grandmother said. "The mercy of it was Martha Elizabeth."

She still had more to tell, but she paused again, and again she looked at me and touched my hand.

"If God loves the ones we can't," she said, "then finally maybe we can. All these years I've thought of him sitting in those shadows, with Martha Elizabeth standing there, and his work-sore old hands over his face."

Once the body of Ben Feltner was laid on his bed, the men who had helped Jack to carry him home went quietly out through the kitchen and the back door, as they had come in, muttering or nodding their commiseration in response to Nancy's "Thank you." And Jack stayed. He stayed to be within sight or call of his sister when she needed him, and he stayed to keep his eye on Mat. Their struggle in front of Chatham's store, Jack knew, had changed them both. Because he did not yet know how or how much or if it was complete, it was not yet a change that he was willing, or that he dared, to turn his back on.

Someone was sent to take word to Rebecca Finley, Margaret's mother, and to ask her to come for Bess.

When Rebecca came, Margaret brought Bess down the stairs into the quiet that the women now did their best to disguise. But Bess, who did not know what was wrong and who tactfully allowed the pretense that nothing was, knew nevertheless that the habits of the house were now broken, and she had heard the quiet that she would never forget.

"Grandma Finley is here to take you home with her," Margaret said, giving her voice the lilt of cheerfulness. "You've been talking about going to stay with her, haven't you?"

And Bess said, dutifully supplying the smile she felt her mother wanted, "Yes."

"We're going to bake some cookies just as soon as we get home," Rebecca said. "Do you want to bake a gingerbread boy?"

"Yes," Bess said.

She removed her hand from her mother's hand and placed it in her grandmother's. They went out the door.

The quiet returned. From then on, though there was much that had to be done and the house stayed full of kin and neighbors coming and going or staying to help, and though by midafternoon women were already bringing food, the house preserved a quiet against all sound. No voice was raised. No door was slammed. Everybody moved as if in consideration, not of each other, but of the quiet itself—as if the quiet denoted some fragile peacefulness in Ben's new sleep that should not be intruded upon.

Jack Beechum was party to that quiet. He made no sound. He said nothing, for his own silence had become wonderful to him and he could not bear to break it. Though Nancy, after the death of their mother, had given Jack much of his upbringing and had been perhaps more his mother than his sister, Ben had never presumed to be a father to him. From the time Jack was eight years old, Ben had been simply his friend—had encouraged, instructed, corrected, helped, and stood by him; had placed a kindly, humorous, forbearing expectation upon him that he could not shed or shirk and had at last lived up to. They had been companions. And yet, through the rest of that day, Jack had his mind more on Mat than on Ben.

Jack watched Mat as he would have watched a newborn

colt weak on its legs that he had helped to stand, that might continue to stand or might not. All afternoon Jack did not sit down because Mat did not. Sometimes there were things to do, and they were busy. Space for the coffin had to be made in the living room. Furniture had to be moved. When the time came, the laden coffin had to be moved into place. But, busy or not, Mat was almost constantly moving, as if seeking his place in a world newly made that day, a world still shaking and doubtful underfoot. And Jack both moved with him and stayed apart from him, watching. When they spoke again, they would speak on different terms.

There was a newness in the house, a solemnity, a sort of wariness, a restlessness as of a dog uneasy on the scent of some creature undeniably present but unknown. In its quiet, the house seemed to be straining to accommodate Ben's absence, made undeniable and insistent by the presence of his body lying still under his folded hands.

Jack would come later to his own reckoning with that loss, the horror and the pity of it, and the grief, the awe and gratitude and love and sorrow and regret, when Ben, newly dead and renewing sorrow for others dead before, would wholly occupy his mind in the night, and could give no comfort, and would not leave. But now Jack stayed by Mat and helped as he could.

In the latter part of the afternoon came Della Budge, Miss Della, bearing an iced cake on a stand like a lighted lamp. As she left the kitchen and started for the front door, she laid her eyes on Jack, who was standing in the door between the living room and the hall. She was a large woman, far gone in years. It was a labor for her to walk. She advanced each foot ahead of the other with care, panting, her hand on her hip, rocking from side to side. She wore many clothes, for her blood was thin and she was easily chilled, and she carried a fan, for sometimes she got too warm. Her little dustcap struggled to stay on top of her head. A tiny pair of spectacles perched awry on her nose. She had a face like a shriveled apple, and the creases at the corners of her mouth were stained with snuff. Once, she had been Jack's teacher. For years they had waged a contest in which she had endeavored to teach him the begats from Abraham to Jesus and he had refused to learn them. He was one of her failures, but she maintained a proprietary interest in him nonetheless. She was the only one left alive who called him "Jackie."

As she came up to him he said, "Hello, Miss Della."

"Well, Jackie," she said, lifting and canting her nose to bring her spectacles to bear upon him, "poor Ben has met his time."

"Yes, mam," Jack said. "One of them things."

"When your time comes you must go, by the hand of man or the stroke of God."

"Yes, mam," Jack said. He was standing with his hands behind him, leaning back against the doorjamb.

"It'll come by surprise," she said. "It's a time appointed, but we'll not be notified."

Jack said he knew it. He did know it.

"So we must always be ready," she said. "Pray without ceasing."

"Yes, mam."

"Well, God bless Ben Feltner. He was a good man. God rest his soul."

Jack stepped ahead of her to help her out the door and down the porch steps.

"Why, thank you, Jackie," she said as she set foot at last on the walk.

He stood and watched her going away, walking, it seemed to him, a tottering edge between eternity and time.

Toward evening Margaret laid the table, and the family and several of the neighbor women gathered in the kitchen. Only two or three men had come, and they were sitting in the living room by the coffin. The table was spread with the abundance of food that had been brought in. They were just preparing to sit down when the murmur of voices they had been hearing from the road down in front of the stores seemed to converge and to move in their direction. Those in the kitchen stood and listened a moment, and then Mat started for the front of the house. The others followed him through the hall and out onto the porch.

The sun was down, the light cool and directionless, so that the colors of the foliage and of the houses and storefronts of the town seemed to glow. Chattering swifts circled and swerved above the chimneys. Nothing else moved except the crowd that made its way at an almost formal pace into the yard. The people standing on the porch were as still as everything else, except for Jack Beechum who quietly made his way forward until he stood behind and a little to the left of Mat, who was standing at the top of the steps.

The crowd moved up near the porch and stopped. There was a moment of hesitation while it murmured and jostled inside itself.

"Be quiet, boys," somebody said. "Let Doc do the talking."

They became still, and then Doctor Starns, who stood in the front rank, took a step forward.

"Mat," he said, "we're here as your daddy's friends. We've got word that Thad Coulter's locked up in the jail at Hargrave. We want you to know that we don't like what he did."

Several voices said, "No!" and "Nosir!"

"We know it was a thing done out of meanness. We don't think we can stand for it, or that we ought to, or that we ought to wait on somebody else's opinion about it. He was seen by a large number of witnesses to do what he did."

Somebody said, "That's right!"

"We think it's our business, and we propose to make it our business."

"That's right!" said several voices.

"It's only up to you to say the word, and we'll ride down there tonight and put justice beyond question. We have a rope."

And in the now-silent crowd someone held up a coil of rope, a noose already tied.

The doctor gave a slight bow of his head to Mat and then tipped his hat to Nancy who now stood behind Mat and to his right. And again the crowd murmured and slightly stirred within itself.

For what seemed to Jack a long time, Mat did not

speak or move. The crowd grew quiet again, and again they could hear the swifts chittering in the air. Jack's right hand ached to reach out to Mat. It seemed to him again that he felt the earth shaking under his feet, as Mat felt it. But though it shook and though they felt it, Mat now stood resolved and calm upon it. Looking at the back of his head, Jack could still see the boy in him, but the head was up. The voice, when it came, was steady:

"No, gentlemen. I appreciate it. We all do. But I ask you not to do it."

And Jack, who had not sat down since morning, stepped back and sat down.

Nancy, under whose feet the earth was not shaking, if it ever had, stepped up beside her son and took his arm.

She said to the crowd, "I know you are my husband's friends. I thank you. I, too, must ask you not to do as you propose. Mat has asked you; I have asked you; if Ben could, he would ask you. Let us make what peace is left for us to make."

"If you want to," Mat said, "come and be with us. We have food, and you all are welcome."

He had said, in all, six brief sentences. He was not a forward man. This, I think, was the only public speech of his life.

"I can see him yet," my grandmother said, her eyes, full of sudden moisture, again turned to the window. "I wish you could have seen him."

And now, after so many years, perhaps I have. I have sought that moment out, or it has sought me, and I see him standing without prop in the deepening twilight, asking his father's friends to renounce the vengeance that a few hours before he himself had been furious to exact.

This is the man who will be my grandfather—the man who will be the man who was my grandfather. The tenses slur and slide under the pressure of collapsed time. For that moment on the porch is not a now that was but a now that is and will be, inhabiting all the history of Port William that followed and will follow. I know that in the days after his father's death—and after Thad Coulter, concurring in the verdict of his would-be jury in Port William, hung himself in the Hargrave jail and so released Martha Elizabeth from her watch—my grandfather renewed and carried on his friendship with the Coulters: with Thad's widow and daughters, with Dave Coulter and his family, and with another first cousin of Thad's, Marce Catlett, my grandfather on my father's side. And when my father asked leave of the Feltners to marry their daughter Bess, my mother, he was made welcome.

Mat Feltner dealt with Ben's murder by not talking about it and thus keeping it in the past. In his last years, I liked to get him to tell me about the violent old times of the town, the hard drinking and the fighting. And he would oblige me up to a point, enjoying the outrageous old stories himself, I think. But always there would come a time in the midst of the telling when he would become silent, shake his head, lift one hand and let it fall; and I would know—I know better now than I did then—that he had remembered his father's death.

Though Coulters still abound in Port William, no Feltner of the name is left. But the Feltner line continues, joined to the Coulter line, in me, and I am here. I am blood kin to both sides of that moment when Ben Feltner turned to face Thad Coulter in the road and Thad pulled the trigger. The two families, sundered in the ruin of a friendship, were united again first in new friendship and then in marriage. My grandfather made a peace here that has joined many who would otherwise have been divided. I am the child of his forgiveness.

After Mat spoke the second time, inviting them in, the crowd loosened and came apart. Some straggled back down into the town; others, as Mat had asked, came into the house, where their wives already were.

But Jack did not stay with them. As soon as he knew he was free, his thoughts went to other things. His horse had stood a long time, saddled, without water or feed. The evening chores were not yet done. Ruth would be wondering what had happened. In the morning they would come back together, to be of use if they could. And there would be, for Jack as for the others, the long wearing out of grief. But now he could stay no longer.

As soon as the porch was cleared, he retrieved his hat from the hall tree and walked quietly out across the yard under the maples and the descending night. So as not to be waylaid by talk, he walked rapidly down the middle of the road to where he had tied his horse. Lamps had now been lighted in the stores and the houses. As he approached, his horse nickered to him.

"I know it," Jack said.

As soon as the horse felt his rider's weight on the stirrup, he started. Soon the lights and noises of the town were behind them, and there were only a few stars, a low red streak in the west, and the horse's eager footfalls on the road.

A Jonquil
for Mary Penn

Mary Penn was sick, though she said nothing about it when she heard Elton get up and light the lamp and renew the fires. He dressed and went out with the lantern to milk and feed and harness the team. It was early March, and she could hear the wind blowing, rattling things. She threw the covers off and sat up on the side of the bed, feeling as she did how easy it would be to let her head lean down again onto her knees. But she got up, put on her dress and sweater, and went to the kitchen.

Nor did she mention it when Elton came back in, bringing the milk, with the smell of the barn cold in his clothes.

"How're you this morning?" he asked her, giving her a pat as she strained the milk.

And she said, not looking at him, for she did not want him to know how she felt, "Just fine."

He ate hungrily the eggs, sausage, and biscuits that she set in front of him, twice emptying the glass that he replenished from a large pitcher of milk. She loved to watch him eat—there was something curiously delicate in the way he used his large hands—but this morning she busied herself about the kitchen, not looking at him, for she knew he was watching her. She had not even set a place for herself.

"You're not hungry?" he asked.

"Not very. I'll eat something after while."

He put sugar and cream in his coffee and stirred rapidly with the spoon. Now he lingered a little. He did not indulge himself often, but this was one of his moments of leisure. He gave himself to his pleasures as concentratedly as to his work. He was never partial about anything; he never felt two ways at the same time. It was, she thought, a kind of childishness in him. When he was happy, he was entirely happy, and he could be as entirely sad or angry. His glooms were the darkest she had ever seen. He worked as a hungry dog ate, and yet he could play at croquet or cards with the self-forgetful exuberance of a little boy. It was for his concentratedness, she supposed, if such a thing could be supposed about, that she loved him. That and her yen just to look at him, for it was wonderful to her the way he was himself in his slightest look or gesture. She did not understand him in everything he did, and yet she recognized him in everything he did. She had not been prepared—she was hardly prepared yet—for the assent she had given to him.

Though he might loiter a moment over his coffee, the day, she knew, had already possessed him; its momentum was on him. When he rose from bed in the morning, he stepped into the day's work, impelled into it by the tension, never apart from him, between what he wanted to do and what he could do. The little hillside place that they had rented from his mother afforded him no proper scope for his ability and desire. They always needed money, but, day by day, they were getting by. Though the times were hard, they were not going to be in want. But she knew his need to surround her with a margin of pleasure and ease. This was his need, not hers; still, when he was not working at home, he would be working, or looking for work, for pay.

This morning, delaying his own plowing, he was going to help Walter Cotman plow his corn ground. She could feel the knowledge of what he had to do tightening in him like a spring. She thought of him and Walter plowing, starting in the early light, and the two teams leaning into the collars all day, while the men walked in the opening furrows, and the steady wind shivered the dry grass, shook the dead weeds, and rattled the treetops in the woods.

He stood and pushed in his chair. She came to be hugged as she knew he wanted her to.

"It's mean out," he said. "Stay in today. Take some care of yourself."

"You, too," she said. "Have you got on plenty of clothes?"

"When I get 'em all on, I will." He was already wearing an extra shirt and a pair of overalls over his corduroys. Now he put on a sweater, his work jacket, his cap and gloves. He started out the door and then turned back. "Don't worry about the chores. I'll be back in time to do everything."

"All right," she said.

He shut the door. And now the kitchen was a cell of still lamplight under the long wind that passed without inflection over the ridges.

She cleared the table. She washed the few dishes he had dirtied and put them away. The kitchen contained the table and four chairs, and the small dish cabinet that they had bought, and the large iron cookstove that looked more permanent than the house. The stove, along with the bed and a few other sticks of furniture, had been there when they came.

She heard Elton go by with the team, heading out the lane. The daylight would be coming now, though the windowpanes still reflected the lamplight. She took the broom from its corner by the back door and swept and tidied up the room. They had been able to do nothing to improve the house, which had never been a good one and had seen hard use. The wallpaper, and probably the plaster behind, had cracked in places. The finish had worn off the linoleum rugs near the doorways and around the stoves. But she kept the house clean. She had made curtains. The curtains in the kitchen were of the same blue-and-white checkered gingham as the tablecloth. The bed stands were orange crates for which she had made skirts of the same cloth. Though the house was poor and hard to keep, she had made it neat and homey. It was her first house, and usually it made her happy. But not now.

She was sick. At first it was a consolation to her to have the whole day to herself to be sick in. But by the time she got the kitchen straightened up, even that small happiness had left her. She had a fever, she guessed, for every motion she made seemed to carry her uneasily beyond the vertical. She had a floaty feeling that made her unreal to herself. And finally, when she put the broom away, she let herself sag down into one of the chairs at the table. She ached. She was overpoweringly tired.

She had rarely been sick and never since she married. And now she did something else that was unlike her: she allowed herself to feel sorry for herself. She remembered that she and Elton had quarreled the night before—about what, she could not remember; perhaps it was not rememberable; perhaps she did not know. She remembered the heavy, mostly silent force of his anger. It had been only another of those tumultuous darknesses that came over him as suddenly and sometimes as unaccountably as a July storm. She was miserable, she told herself. She was sick and alone. And perhaps the sorrow that she felt for herself was not altogether unjustified.

She and Elton had married a year and a half earlier, when she was seventeen and he eighteen. She had never seen anybody like him. He had a wild way of rejoicing, like a healthy child, singing songs, joking, driving his old car as if he were drunk and the road not wide enough. He could make her weak with laughing at him. And yet he was already a man as few men were. He had been making his own living since he was fourteen, when he had quit school. His father had been dead by then for five years. He had hated his stepfather. When a neighbor had offered him crop ground, room, and wages, he had taken charge of himself and, though he was still a boy, he had become a man. He wanted, he said, to have to say thank you to nobody. Or to nobody but her. He would be glad, he said with a large grin, to say thank you to her. And he could *do* things. It was wonderful what he could accomplish with those enormous hands of his. She could have put her hand into his and walked right off the edge of the world. Which, in a way, is what she did.

She had grown up in a substantial house on a good upland farm. Her family was not wealthy, but it was an old family, proud of itself, always conscious of its position and of its responsibility to be itself. She had known from childhood that she would be sent to college. Almost from childhood she had understood that she was destined to be married to a solid professional man, a doctor perhaps, or (and this her mother particularly favored) perhaps a minister.

And so when she married Elton she did so without telling her family. She already knew their judgment of Elton: "He's nothing." She and Elton simply drove down to Hargrave one late October night, awakened a preacher, and got married, hoping that their marriage would be accepted as an accomplished fact. They were wrong. It was not acceptable, and it was never going to be. She no longer belonged in that house, her parents told her.

She no longer belonged to that family. To them it would be as if she had never lived.

She was seventeen, she had attended a small denominational college for less than two months, and now her life as it had been had ended. The day would come when she would know herself to be a woman of faith. Now she merely loved and trusted. Nobody was living then on Elton's mother's little farm on Cotman Ridge, where Elton had lived for a while when he was a child. They rented the place and moved in, having just enough money to pay for the new dish cabinet and the table and four chairs. Elton, as it happened, already owned a milk cow in addition to his team and a few tools.

It was a different world, a new world to her, that she came into then—a world of poverty and community. They were in a neighborhood of six households, counting their own, all within half a mile of one another. Besides themselves there were Braymer and Josie Hardy and their children; Tom Hardy and his wife, also named Josie; Walter and Thelma Cotman and their daughter, Irene; Jonah and Daisy Hample and their children; and Uncle Isham and Aunt Frances Quail, who were Thelma Cotman's and Daisy Hample's parents. The two Josies, to save confusion, were called Josie Braymer and Josie Tom. Josie Tom was Walter Cotman's sister. In the world that Mary Penn had given up, a place of far larger and richer farms, work was sometimes exchanged, but the families were conscious of themselves in a way that set them apart from one another. Here, in this new world, neighbors were always working together. "Many hands make light work," Uncle Isham Quail loved to say, though his own old hands were no longer able to work much.

Some work only the men did together, like haying and harvesting the corn. Some work only the women did together: sewing or quilting or wallpapering or house-cleaning; and whenever the men were together working, the women would be together cooking. Some work the men and women did together: harvesting tobacco or killing hogs or any other job that needed many hands. It was an old community. They all had worked together a long time. They all knew what each one was good at. When they worked together, not much needed to be explained. When they went down to the little weather-boarded church at Goforth on Sunday morning, they were glad to see one another and had much to say, though they had seen each other almost daily during the week.

This neighborhood opened to Mary and Elton and took them in with a warmth that answered her parents' rejection. The men, without asking or being asked, included Elton in whatever they were doing. They told him when and where they needed him. They came to him when he needed them. He was an apt and able hand, and they were glad to have his help. He learned from them all but liked best to work with Walter Cotman, who was a fine farmer. He and Walter were, up to a point, two of a kind; both were impatient of disorder—"I can't stand a damned mess," said Walter, and he made none—and both loved the employment of their minds in their work. They were unlike in that Walter was satisfied within the boundaries of his little farm, but Elton could not have been. Nonetheless, Elton loved his growing understanding of Walter's character and his ways. Though he was a quiet man and gave neither instruction nor advice, Walter was Elton's teacher, and Elton was consciously his student.

Once, when they had killed hogs and Elton and Mary had stayed at home to finish rendering their lard, the boiling fat had foamed up and begun to run over the sides of the kettle. Mary ran to the house and called Walter on the party line.

"Tell him to throw the fire to it," Walter said. "Tell him to dip out some lard and throw it on the fire."

Elton did so, unbelieving, but the fire flared, grew hotter, the foaming lard subsided in the kettle, and Elton's face relaxed from anxiety and self-accusation into a grin. "Well," he said, quoting Walter in Walter's voice, "it's all in knowing how."

Mary, who had more to learn than Elton, became a daughter to every woman in the community. She came knowing little, barely enough to begin, and they taught her much. Thelma, Daisy, and the two Josies taught her their ways of cooking, cleaning, and sewing; they taught her to can, pickle, and preserve; they taught her to do the women's jobs in the hog killing. They took her on their expeditions to one another's houses to cook harvest meals or to houseclean or to gather corn from the fields and can it. One day they all walked down to Goforth to do some wallpapering for Josie Tom's mother. They papered two rooms, had a good time, and Josie Tom's mother fixed them a dinner of fried chicken, creamed new potatoes and peas, hot biscuits, and cherry cobbler.

In cold weather they sat all afternoon in one another's houses, quilting or sewing or embroidering. Josie Tom was the best at needlework. Everything she made was a wonder. From spring to fall, for a Christmas present for someone, she always embroidered a long cloth that began with the earliest flowers of spring and ended with the last flowers of fall. She drew the flowers on the cloth with a pencil and worked them in with her needle and colored threads. She included the flowers of the woods and fields, the dooryards and gardens. She loved to point to the penciled outlines and name the flowers as if calling them up in their beauty into her imagination. "Look-a-there," she would say. "I even put in a jimsonweed." "And a bull thistle," said Tom Hardy, who had his doubts about weeds and thistles but was proud of her for leaving nothing out.

Josie Tom was a plump, pretty, happy woman, childless but the mother of any child in reach. Mary Penn loved her the best, perhaps, but she loved them all. They were only in their late thirties or early forties, but to Mary they seemed to belong to the ageless, eternal generation of mothers, unimaginably older and more experienced than herself. She called them Miss Josie, Miss Daisy, and Miss Thelma. They warmed and sheltered her. Sometimes she could just have tossed herself at them like a little girl to be hugged.

They were capable, unasking, generous, humorous women, and sometimes, among themselves, they were raucous and free, unlike the other women she had known. On their way home from picking blackberries one afternoon, they had to get through a new barbed wire fence. Josie Tom held two wires apart while the other four gathered their skirts, leaned down, and straddled through.

Josie Tom handed their filled buckets over. And then Josie Braymer held the wires apart, and Josie Tom, stooping through, got the back of her dress hung on the top wire.

"I *knew* it!" she said, and she began to laugh.

They all laughed, and nobody laughed more than Josie Tom, who was standing spraddled and stooped, helpless to move without tearing her dress.

"Josie Braymer," she said, "are you going to just stand there, or are you going to unhook me from this shitten fence?"

And there on the ridgetop in the low sunlight they danced the dance of women laughing, bending and straightening, raising and lowering their hands, swaying and stepping with their heads back.

Daylight was full in the windows now. Mary made herself get up and extinguish the lamp on the table. The lamps all needed to be cleaned and trimmed and refilled, and she had planned to do that today. The whole house needed to be dusted and swept. And she had mending to do. She tied a scarf around her head, put on her coat, and went out.

Only day before yesterday it had been spring—warm, sunny, and still. Elton said the wildflowers were starting up in the leafless woods, and she found a yellow crocus in the yard. And then this dry and bitter wind had come, driving down from the north as if it were as long and wide as time, and the sky was as gray as if the sun had never shone. The wind went through her coat, pressed her fluttering skirt tight against her legs, tore at her scarf. It chilled her to the bone. She went first to the privy in a back corner of the yard and then on to the henhouse, where she shelled corn for the hens and gave them fresh water.

On her way back to the house she stood a moment, looking off in the direction in which she knew Elton and Walter Cotman were plowing. By now they would have accepted even this day as it was; by now they might have shed their jackets. Later they would go in and wash and sit down in Thelma's warm kitchen for their dinner, hungry, glad to be at rest for a little while before going back again to work through the long afternoon. Though they were not far away, though she could see them in her mind's eye, their day and hers seemed estranged, divided by great distance and long time. She was cold, and the wind's insistence wearied her; the wind was like a living creature, rearing and pressing against her so that she might have cried out to it in exasperation, "*What* do you *want?*"

When she got back into the house, she was shivering, her teeth chattering. She unbuttoned her coat without taking it off and sat down close to the stove. They heated only two rooms, the kitchen and the front room where they slept. The stove in the front room might be warmer, she thought, and she could sit in the rocking chair by it; but having already sat down, she did not get up. She had much that she needed to be doing, she told herself. She ought at least to get up and make the bed. And she wanted to tend to the lamps; it always pleased her to have them clean. But she did not get up. The stove's heat drove the cold out of her clothes, and gradually her shivering stopped.

They had had a hard enough time of it their first winter. They had no fuel, no food laid up. Elton had raised a crop but no garden. He borrowed against the crop to buy a meat hog. He cut and hauled in firewood. He worked for wages to buy groceries, but the times were hard and he could not always find work. Sometimes their meals consisted of biscuits and a gravy made of lard and flour.

And yet they were often happy. Often the world afforded them something to laugh about. Elton stayed alert for anything that was funny and brought the stories home. He told her how the tickle-ass grass got into Uncle Isham's pants, and how Daisy Hample clucked to her nearsighted husband and children like a hen with half-grown chicks, and how Jonah Hample, missing the steps, walked off the edge of Braymer Hardy's front porch, fell into a rosebush, and said, "Now, I didn't go to do that!" Elton could make the funny things happen again in the dark as they lay in bed at night; sometimes they would laugh until their eyes were wet with tears. When they got snowed in that winter, they would drive the old car down the hill until it stalled in the drifts, and drag it out with the team, and ram it into the drifts again, laughing until the horses looked at them in wonder.

When the next year came, they began at the beginning, and though the times had not improved, they improved themselves. They bought a few hens and a rooster from Josie Braymer. They bought a second cow. They put in a garden. They bought two shoats to raise for meat. Mary learned to preserve the food they would need for winter.

When the cows freshened, she learned to milk. She took a small bucket of cream and a few eggs to Port William every Saturday night and used the money she made to buy groceries and to pay on their debts.

Slowly she learned to imagine where she was. The ridge named for Walter Cotman's family is a long one, curving out toward the river between the two creek valleys of Willow Run and Katie's Branch. As it comes near to the river valley it gets narrower, its sides steeper and more deeply incised by hollows. When Elton and Mary Penn were making their beginning there, the uplands were divided into many farms, few of which contained as much as a hundred acres. The hollows, the steeper hillsides, the bluffs along the sides of the two creek valleys were covered with thicket or woods. From where the hawks saw it, the ridge would have seemed a long, irregular promontory reaching out into a sea of trees. And it bore on its back crisscrossings of other trees along the stone or rail or wire fences, trees in thickets and groves, trees in the houseyards. And on rises of ground or tucked into folds were the gray, paintless buildings of the farmsteads, connected to one another by lanes and paths. Now she thought of herself as belonging there, not just because of her marriage to Elton but also because of the economy that the two of them had made around themselves and with their neighbors. She had learned to think of herself as living and working at the center of a wonderful provisioning: the kitchen and garden, hog pen and smokehouse, henhouse and cellar of her own household; the little commerce of giving and taking that spoked out along the paths connecting her household to the others; Port William on its ridgetop in one direction, Goforth in its valley in the other; and all this at the heart of the weather and the world.

On a bright, still day in the late fall, after all the leaves were down, she had stood on the highest point and had seen the six smokes of the six houses rising straight up into the wide downfalling light. She knew which smoke came from which house. It was like watching the rising up of prayers or some less acknowledged communication between Earth and Heaven. She could not say to herself how it made her feel.

She loved her jars of vegetables and preserves on the cellar shelves, and the potato bin beneath, the cured hams and shoulders and bacons hanging in the smokehouse, the two hens already brooding their clutches of marked eggs, the egg basket and the cream bucket slowly filling, week after week. But today these things seemed precious and far away, as if remembered from another world or another life. Her sickness made things seem arbitrary and awry. Nothing had to be the way it was. As easily as she could see the house as it was, she could imagine it empty, windowless, the tin roof blowing away, the chimneys crumbling, the cellar caved in, weeds in the yard. She could imagine Elton and herself gone, and the rest of them—Hardy, Hample, Cotman, and Quail—gone too.

Elton could spend an hour telling her—and himself—how Walter Cotman went about his work. Elton was a man fascinated with farming, and she could see him picking his way into it with his understanding. He wanted to know the best ways of doing things. He wanted to see how a way of doing came out of a way of thinking and a way of living. He was interested in the ways people talked and wore their clothes.

The Hamples were another of his studies. Jonah Hample and his young ones were almost useless as farmers because, as Elton maintained, they could not see all the way to the ground. They did not own a car because they could not see well enough to drive—"They need to drive something with eyes," Elton said—and yet they were all born mechanics. They could fix anything. While Daisy Hample stood on the porch clucking about the weeds in their crops, Jonah and his boys and sometimes his girls, too, would be busy with some machine that somebody had brought for them to fix. The Hample children went about the neighborhood in a drove, pushing a fairly usable old bicycle that they loved but could not ride.

Elton watched Braymer, too. Unlike his brother and Walter Cotman, Braymer liked to know what was going on in the world. Like the rest of them, Braymer had no cash to spare, but he liked to think about what he would do with money if he had it. He liked knowing where something could be bought for a good price. He liked to hear what somebody had done to make a little money and then to think about it and tell the others about it while they worked. "Braymer would be a trader if he had a chance," Elton told Mary. "He'd like to try a little of this and a little of that, and see how he did with it. Walter and Tom like what they've got."

"And you don't like what you've got," Mary said.

He grinned big at her, as he always did when she read his mind. "I like some of it," he said.

At the end of the summer, when she and Elton were beginning their first tobacco harvest in the neighborhood, Tom Hardy said to Elton, "Now, Josie Braymer can out-cut us all, Elton. If she gets ahead of you, just don't pay it any mind."

"Tom," Elton said, "I'm going to leave here now and go to the other end of this row. If Josie Braymer's there when I get there, I'm going home."

When he got there Josie Braymer was not there, and neither was any of the men. It was not that he did not want to be bested by a woman; he did not want to be bested by anybody. One thing Mary would never have to do was wonder which way he was. She knew he would rather die than be beaten. It was maybe not the best way to be, she thought, but it was the way he was, and she loved him. It was both a trouble and a comfort to her to know that he would always require the most of himself. And he was beautiful, the way he moved in his work. It stirred her.

She could feel ambition constantly pressing in him. He could do more than he had done, and he was always looking for the way. He was like an axman at work in a tangled thicket, cutting and cutting at the brush and the vines and the low limbs, trying to make room for a full swing. For this year he had rented corn ground from Josie Tom's mother down by Goforth, two miles away. When he went down with his team to work, he would have to take his dinner. It would mean more work for them both, but he was desperate for room to exert himself.

They were poor as the times, they saw more obstacles than openings, and yet she believed without doubt that Elton was on his way.

It was not his ambition—his constant, tireless, often exhilarated preoccupation with work—that troubled her. She could stay with him in that. She had learned that she could do, and do well and gladly enough, whatever she would have to do. She had no fear. What troubled her were the dark and mostly silent angers that often settled upon him and estranged him from everything. At those times, she knew, he doubted himself, and he suffered and raged in his doubt. He may have been born with this doubt in him, she sometimes imagined; it was as though his soul were like a little moon that would be dark at times and bright at others. But she knew also that her parents' rejection of him had cost him dearly. Even as he defied them to matter to him, they held a power over him that he could not shake off. In his inability to forgive them, he consented to this power, and their rejection stood by him and measured him day by day. Her parents' pride was social, belonging, even in its extremity, to their kind and time. But Elton's pride was merely creaturely, albeit that of an extraordinary creature; it was a creature's naked claim on the right to respect itself, a claim that no creature's life, of itself, could invariably support. At times he seemed to her a man in the light in daily struggle with a man in the dark, and sometimes the man in the dark had the upper hand.

Elton never felt that any mistake was affordable; he and Mary were living within margins that were too narrow. He required perfection of himself. When he failed, he was like the sun in a cloud, alone and burning, furious in his doubt, furious at her because she trusted in him though he doubted. How could she dare to love him, who did not love himself? And then, sometimes accountably, sometimes not, the cloud would move away, and he would light up everything around him. His own force and intelligence would be clear within him then; he would be skillful and joyful, passionate in his love of order, funny and tender.

At his best, Elton was a man in love—with her but not just with her. He was in love too with the world, with their place in the world, with that scanty farm, with his own life, with farming. At those times she lived in his love as in a spacious house.

Walter Cotman always spoke of Mary as Elton's "better half." In spite of his sulks and silences, she would not go so far as "better." That she was his half, she had no doubt at all. He needed her. At times she knew with a joyous ache that she completed him, just as she knew with the same joy that she needed him and he completed her. How beautiful a thing it was, she thought, to be a half, to be completed by such another half! When had there ever been such a yearning of halves toward each other, such a longing, even in quarrels, to be whole? And sometimes they would be whole. Their wholeness came upon them as a rush of light, around them and within them, so that she felt they must be shining in the dark.

But now that wholeness was not imaginable; she felt herself a part without counterpart, a mere fragment of something unknown, dark and broken off. The fire had burned low in the stove. Though she still wore her coat,

she was chilled again and shaking. For a long time, perhaps, she had been thinking of nothing, and now misery
alerted her again to the room. The wind ranted and
sucked at the house's corners. She could hear its billows
and shocks, as if somebody off in the distance were shaking a great rug. She felt, not a draft, but the whole at-
mosphere of the room moving coldly against her. She
went into the other room, but the fire there also needed
building up. She could not bring herself to do it. She was
shaking, she ached, she could think only of lying down.
Standing near the stove, she undressed, put on her nightgown again, and went to bed.

She lay chattering and shivering while the bedclothes
warmed around her. It seemed to her that a time might
come when sickness would be a great blessing, for she
truly did not care if she died. She thought of Elton, caught
up in the day's wind, who could not even look at her
and see that she was sick. If she had not been too miserable, she would have cried. But then her thoughts began
to slip away, like dishes sliding along a table pitched as
steeply as a roof. She went to sleep.

When she woke, the room was warm. A teakettle on the
heating stove was muttering and steaming. Though the
wind was still blowing hard, the room was full of sunlight.
The lamp on the narrow mantel shelf behind the stove
was filled and clean, its chimney gleaming, and so was
the one on the stand by the bed. Josie Tom was sitting
in the rocker by the window, sunlight flowing in on the
unfinished long embroidery she had draped over her lap.

She was bowed over her work, filling in with her needle and a length of yellow thread the bright corolla of a jonquil—or "Easter lily," as she would have called it. She was humming the tune of an old hymn, something she often did while she was working, apparently without awareness that she was doing it. Her voice was resonant, low, and quiet, barely audible, as if it were coming out of the air and she, too, were merely listening to it. The yellow flower was nearly complete.

And so Mary knew all the story of her day. Elton, going by Josie Tom's in the half-light, had stopped and called.

She could hear his voice, raised to carry through the wind: "Mrs. Hardy, Mary's sick, and I have to go over to Walter's to plow."

So he had known. He had thought of her. He had told Josie Tom.

Feeling herself looked at, Josie Tom raised her head and smiled. "Well, are you awake? Are you all right?"

"Oh, I'm wonderful," Mary said. And she slept again.

3

Making It Home

He had crossed the wide ocean and many a river. Now not another river lay between him and home but only a few creeks that he knew by name. Arthur Rowanberry had come a long way, trusting somebody else to know where he was, and now he knew where he was himself. The great river, still raised somewhat from the flood of that spring and flowing swiftly, lay off across the fields to his left; to his right and farther away were the wooded slopes of the Kentucky side of the valley, and over it all, from the tops of the hills on one side to the tops of the hills on the other, stretched the gray sky. He was walking along the blacktop that followed the river upstream to the county seat of Hargrave. On the higher ground to the right of the road stood fine brick farmhouses that had been built a hundred and more years ago from the earnings of the rich bottomland fields that lay around them. There had been a time when those houses had seemed as permanent to him as the land they stood on. But where he had been, they had the answer to such houses.

"We wouldn't let one of them stand long in our way," he thought.

Art Rowanberry walked like the first man to discover upright posture—as if, having been a creature no taller than a sheep or a pig, he had suddenly risen to the height of six feet and looked around. He walked too like a man who had been taught to march, and he wore a uniform. But whatever was military in his walk was an overlay, like the uniform, for he had been a man long before he had been a soldier, and a farmer long before he had been a man. An observer might have sensed in his walk and in the way he carried himself a reconciliation to the forms and distances of the land such as comes only to those who have from childhood been accustomed to the land's work.

The noises of the town were a long way behind him. It was too early for the evening chores, and the farmsteads that he passed were quiet. Birds sang. From time to time he heard a farmer call out to his team. Once he had heard a tractor off somewhere in the fields and once a towboat out on the river, but those sounds had faded away. No car had passed him, though he walked a paved main road. There was no sound near him but the sound of his own footsteps falling steadily on the pavement.

Once it had seemed to him that he walked only on the place where he was. But now, having gone and returned from so far, he knew that he was walking on the whole round world. He felt the great, empty distance that the world was turning in, far away from the sun and the moon and the stars.

"Here," he thought, "is where we do what we are going to do—the only chance we got. And if somebody was to be looking down from up there, it would all look a lot littler to him than it does to us."

He was talking carefully to himself in his thoughts, forming the words more deliberately than if he were saying them aloud, because he did not want to count his steps. He had a long way still to go, and he did not want to know how many steps it was going to take. Nor did he want to hear in his head the counted cadence of marching.

"I ain't marching," he thought. "I am going somewheres. I am going up the river towards Hargrave. And this side of Hargrave, before the bridge, at Ellville, I will turn up the Kentucky River, and go ten miles, and turn up Sand Ripple below Port William, and I will be at home."

He carried a duffel bag that contained his overcoat, a change of clothes, and a shaving kit. From time to time, he shifted the bag from one shoulder to the other.

"I reckon I am done marching, have marched my last step, and now I am walking. There is nobody in front of me and nobody behind. I have come here without a by-your-leave to anybody. Them that have known where I was, or was supposed to, for three years don't know where I am now. Nobody that I know knows where I am now."

He came from killing. He had felt the ground shaken by men and what they did. Where he was coming from, they thought about killing day after day, and feared it, and did it. And out of the unending, unrelenting great noise and tumult of the killing went little deaths that belonged to people one by one. Some had feared it and had died. Some had died without fearing it, lacking the time. They had fallen around him until he was amazed that he stood—men who in a little while had become his buddies, most of them younger than he, just boys.

The fighting had been like work, only a lot of people got killed and a lot of things got destroyed. It was not work that *made* much of anything. You and your people intended to go your way, if you could. And you wanted to stop the other people from going their way, if you could. And whatever interfered you destroyed. You had a thing on your mind that you wanted, or wanted to get to, and anything at all that stood in your way, you had the right to destroy. If what was in the way were women and little children, you would not even know it, and it was all the same. When your power is in a big gun, you don't have any small intentions. Whatever you want to hit, you want to make dust out of it. Farms, houses, whole towns—things that people had made well and cared for a long time—you made nothing of.

"We blew them apart and scattered the pieces so they

couldn't be put back together again. And people, too. We blew them apart and scattered the pieces."

He had seen tatters of human flesh hanging in the limbs of trees along with pieces of machines. He had seen bodies without heads, arms and legs without bodies, strewn around indifferently as chips. He had seen the bodies of men hanging upside down from a tank turret, lifeless as dolls.

Once, when they were firing their gun, the man beside him—Eckstrom—began to dance. And Art thought, "This ain't no time to be dancing." But old Eckstrom was dancing because he was shot in the head, was killed, his body trying on its own to keep standing.

And others had gone down, near enough to Art almost that he could have touched them as they fell: Jones, Bitmer, Hirsch, Walters, Corelli.

He had seen attackers coming on, climbing over the bodies of those who had fallen ahead of them. A man who, in one moment, had been a helper, a friend, in the next moment was only a low mound of something in the way, and you stepped over him or stepped on him and came ahead.

Once while they were manning their gun and under fire themselves, old Eckstrom got mad, and he said, "I wish I had those sons of bitches lined up where I could shoot every damned one of them."

And Art said, "Them fellers over there are doing about the same work we are, 'pears like to me."

There were nights when the sky and all the earth appeared to be on fire, and yet the ground was covered with snow and it was cold.

At Christmas he was among those trapped at Bastogne. He had expected to die, but as before he was spared, though the ground shook and the town burned under a sky brighter than day. They held their own, and others, fighting on the outside, broke through.

"We was mighty glad to see that day when it come," he thought. "That was a good day."

The fighting went on, the great tearing apart. People and everything else were torn into pieces. Everything was only pieces put together that were ready to fly apart, and nothing was whole. You got to where you could not look at a man without knowing how little it would take to kill him. For a man was nothing but just a little morsel of soft flesh and brittle bone inside of some clothes. And you could not look at a house or a schoolhouse or a church without knowing how, rightly hit, it would just shake down inside itself into a pile of stones and ashes. There was nothing you could look at that was whole— man or beast or house or tree—that had the right to stay whole very long. There was nothing above the ground that was whole but you had the measure of it and could separate its pieces and bring it down. You moved always in a landscape of death, wreckage, cinders, and snow.

And then, having escaped so far, he was sitting by his artillery piece one afternoon, eating a piece of chocolate and talking to an old redheaded, freckle-faced boy named McBride, and a shell hit right where they were. McBride just disappeared. And a fragment came to Art as if it were his own and had known him from the beginning of the world, and it burrowed into him.

From a man in the light on the outside of the world,

he was transformed in the twinkling of an eye into a man in the dark on the inside of himself, in pain, and he thought that he was dead. How long he was in that darkness he did not know. When he came out of it, he was in a place that was white and clean, a hospital, and he was in a long room with many beds. There was sunlight coming in the window.

A nurse who came by seemed glad to see him. "Well, hello, bright eyes," she said.

He said, "Why, howdy."

She said, "I think the war is over for you, soldier."

"Yes, mam," he said. "I reckon it is."

She patted his shoulder. "You almost got away from us, you know it?"

And he said, "Yes, mam, I expect I did."

The uniform he wore as he walked along the road between Jefferson and Hargrave was now too big for him. His shirt collar was loose on his neck, in spite of the neatly tied tie, and under his tightened belt the waistband of his pants gathered in pleats.

He stayed in hospitals while his life grew back around the wound, as a lightning-struck tree will sometimes heal over the scar, until finally they gave him his papers and let him go.

And now, though he walked strongly enough along the road, he was still newborn from his death, and inside himself he was tender and a little afraid.

The bus had brought him as far as the town of Jefferson on the north side of the river, letting him out in the middle of the afternoon in front of the hotel that served also as a bus station. From there, he could have taken another bus to Hargrave had he been willing to wait until the next morning. But now that he was in familiar country he did not have it in him to wait. He had known a many a man who would have waited, but he was old for a soldier; though he was coming from as far as progress had reached, he belonged to an older time. It did not occur to him, any more than it would have occurred to his grandfather, to wait upon a machine for something he could furnish for himself. And so he thanked the kind lady at the hotel desk, shouldered his bag, and set out for home on foot.

The muddy Ohio flowed beneath the bridge and a flock of pigeons wheeled out and back between the bridge and the water, causing him to sway as he walked, so that to steady himself he had to look at the hills that rose over the rooftops beyond the bridge. He went down the long southward arc of the bridge, and for a little while he was among houses again, and then he was outside the town, walking past farmsteads and fields in unobstructed day. The sky was overcast, but the clouds were high.

"It ought to clear off before morning," he thought. "Maybe it'll be one of them fine spring days. Maybe it'll do to work, for I have got to get started."

They would already have begun plowing, he thought—his father and his brother, Mart. Though they had begun the year without him, they would be expecting him. He could hear his father's voice saying, "Any day now. Any day."

But he was between lives. The war had been a life, such as it was, and now he was out of it. The other life, the one he had once had and would have again, was still ahead of him; he was not in it yet.

He was only free. He had not been out in the country or alone in a long time. Now that he had the open countryside around him again and was alone, he felt the expectations of other people fall away from him like a shed skin, and he came into himself.

"I am not under anybody's orders," he thought. "What I expect myself to do, I will do it. The government don't owe me, and I don't owe it. Except, I reckon, when I have something again that it wants, then I reckon I will owe it."

It pleased him to think that the government owed him nothing, that he needed nothing from it, and he was on his own. But the government seemed to think that it owed him praise. It wanted to speak of what he and the others had done as heroic and glorious. Now that the war was coming to an end, the government wanted to speak of their glorious victories. The government was made up of people who thought about fighting, not of those who did it. The men sitting behind desks—they spent other men to buy ground, and then they ruined the ground they had and more men to get the ground beyond. If they were on the right side, they did it the same as them that were on the wrong side.

"They talk about victory as if they know all them dead boys was glad to die. The dead boys ain't never been asked how glad they was. If they had it to do again, might be they wouldn't do it, or might be they would. But they ain't been asked."

Under the clouds, the country all around was quiet, except for birds singing in the trees, wherever there were trees, and now and then a human voice calling out to a team. He was glad to be alive.

He had been glad to be alive all the time he had been alive. When he was hit and thought he was dead, it had come to him how good it was to be alive even under the shelling, even when it was at its worst. And now he had lived through it all and was coming home. He was now a man who had seen far places and strange things, and he remembered them all. He had seen Kansas and Louisiana and Arizona. He had seen the ocean. He had seen the little farms and country towns of France and Belgium and Luxembourg—pretty, before they were ruined. For one night, he was in Paris.

"That Paris, now. That was something. We was there one day and one night. There was wine everywheres, and these friendly girls who said, 'Kees me.' And I don't know what happened after about ten o'clock. I come to the next morning in this hotel room, sick and broke, with lipstick from one end to the other. I reckon I must have had a right good time."

At first, before he was all the way in it, there was something he liked about the war, a reduction that in a way was pleasing. From a man used to doing and thinking for himself, he became a man who did what he was told.

"That laying around half a day, waiting for somebody else to think—that was something I had to *learn*."

It was fairly restful. Even basic training tired him less than what he would ordinarily have done at that time of year. He gained weight.

And from a man with a farm and crops and stock to worry about, he became a man who worried only about himself and the little bunch of stuff he needed to sleep, dress, eat, and fight.

He furnished only himself. The army furnished what little else it took to make the difference between a man and a beast. More than anything else, he liked his mess kit. It was all the dishes a man really needed. And when you weren't cooking or eating with it, you could keep things in it—a little extra tobacco, maybe.

"When I get to Ellville," he thought, "I won't be but mighty little short of halfway. I know the miles and how they lay out end to end."

It had been evening for a while now. On the farm-steads that he passed, people were busy with the chores. He could hear people calling their stock, dogs barking, children shouting and laughing. On one farm that he passed, a woman, a dog, and a small boy were bringing in the cows; in the driveway of the barn he could see a man unharnessing a team of mules. It was as familiar to him as his breathing, and because he was outside it still, he yearned toward it as a ghost might. As he passed by, the woman, perhaps because he was a soldier, raised her hand to him, and he raised his own in return.

After a while, he could see ahead of him the houses and trees of Ellville, and over the trees the superstructure of the bridge arching into Hargrave. Throughout his walk so far, he had been offering himself the possibility that he would walk on home before he would sleep. But now that he had come nearly halfway and Ellville was in sight, he knew he would not go farther that day. He was tired, and with his tiredness had come a sort of melancholy and a sort of aimlessness, as if, all his ties cut, he might go right on past his home river and on and on, anywhere at all in the world. The little cluster of buildings ahead of him now seemed only accidentally there, and he himself there only accidentally. He had arrived, as he had arrived again and again during the healing of his wound, at the apprehension of a pure emptiness, as if at the center of an explosion—as if, without changing at all, he and the town ahead of him and the village around him and all the long way behind him had been taken up into a dream in which every creature and every thing sat, like old McBride, in the dead center of the possibility of its disappearance.

In the little town a lane turned off the highway and went out beyond the houses and across the river bottom for perhaps a quarter of a mile to a barn and, beyond the barn, to a small weatherboarded church. It was suppertime then; the road and the dooryards were deserted. Art entered the lane and went back past the gardens and the clutter of outbuildings that lay behind the houses. At the barn there was a cistern with a chain pump. He set down his bag and pumped and drank from his cupped left hand held under the spout.

"Looks like I ought to be hungry," he thought. "But I ain't."

He was not hungry, and there was no longer anything much that he wanted to think. He was tired. He told himself to lift the bag again and put it on his shoulder. He told his feet to walk, and they carried him on to the church. The door was unlocked. He went in.

He shut the door behind him, not allowing the latch to click. The quiet inside the church was palpable; he came into it as into a different element, neither air nor water. He crossed the tiny vestibule where a bell rope dangled from a worn hole in the ceiling, went through another door that stood open, and sat down on the first bench to his left, leaving his duffel bag in the aisle, propped against the end of the bench. He let himself become still.

"I will eat a little," he thought, "'gainst I get hungry in the night."

After a while he took a bar of candy from the bag and slowly ate it. The church windows were glazed with an amber-colored glass that you could not see through, and though it was still light outdoors, in the church it was dusk. When he finished the candy, he folded the wrapper soundlessly and put it in his pocket. Taking his overcoat from the bag to use as a blanket, he lay down on the bench. Many thoughts fled by him, none stopping. And then he slept.

He woke several times in the night, listening, and, hearing no threat out in the darkness anywhere, slept again. The last time he woke, roosters were crowing, and he sat up. He sat still a while in the dark, allowing the waking quiet of the place to come over him, and then he took another bar of candy from his bag and ate it and folded the wrapper and put it in his pocket as before. The night chill had seeped into the church; standing, he put on the overcoat. He picked up his bag and felt his way to the door.

It had cleared and the sky was full of stars. To the east, upriver, he could see a faint brightening ahead of the coming day. All around him the dark treetops were throbbing with bird song, and from the banks of the two rivers at their joining, from everywhere there was water, the voices of spring peepers rose as if in clouds. Art stood still and looked around him and listened. It was going to be the fine spring day that he had imagined it might be.

He thought, "If a fellow was to be dead now, and young, might be he would be missing this a long time."

There was a privy in back of the church and he went to it. And then, on his way out of the lane, he stopped at the barn and drank again at the cistern.

Back among the houses, still dark and silent among their trees, he took the road that led up into the smaller of the two river valleys. There was no light yet from the dawn, but by the little light of the stars he could see well enough. All he needed now was the general shape of the place given by various shadows and loomings.

"I have hoofed it home from here a many a night," he thought. "Might be I could do it if I was blind. But I can see."

He could see. And he walked along, feeling the joy of a man who sees, a joy that a man tends to forget in sufficient light. The quiet around him seemed wide as the whole country and deep as the sky, and the morning songs of the creatures and his own footsteps occurred distinctly and separately in it, making a kind of geography and a kind of story. As he walked the light slowly strengthened. As he more and more saw where he was, it seemed to him more and more that he was walking in his memory or that he had entered, awake, a dream that he had been dreaming for a long time.

He was hungry. The candy bar that he had eaten when he woke had hardly interrupted his hunger.

"My belly thinks my throat has been cut. It is laying right flat against my backbone."

It was a joy to him to be so hungry. Hunger had not bothered him much for many weeks, had not mattered, but now it was as vivid to him as a landmark. It was a tree that put its roots into the ground and spread its branches out against the sky.

The east brightened. The sun lit the edges of a few clouds on the horizon and then rose above them. He was walking full in its light. It had not shone on him long before he had to take off the overcoat, and he folded and rolled it neatly and stuffed it into his bag. By then he had come a long way up the road.

Now that it was light, he could see the marks of the flood that had recently covered the valley floor. He could see drift logs and mats of cornstalks that the river had left on the low fields. In places where the river ran near the road, he could see the small clumps of leaves and grasses that the currents had affixed to the tree limbs. Out in one of the bottoms he saw two men with a team and wagon clearing the scattered debris from their fields. They had set fire to a large heap of drift logs, from which the pale smoke rose straight up. Above the level of the flood, the sun shone on the small, still-opening leaves of the water maples and on the short new grass of the hillside pastures.

As he went along, Art began to be troubled about how to present himself to the ones at home. He had not shaved. Since before his long ride on the bus he had not bathed. He did not want to come in, after his three years' absence, like a man coming in from work, unshaven and with his clothes mussed and soiled. He must appear to them as what he had been since they saw him last, a soldier. And then he would be at the end of his soldiering. He did not know yet what he would be when he had ceased to be a soldier, but when he had thought so far his confusion left him.

He came to where the road crossed the mouth of a small tributary valley. Where the stream of that valley passed under the road, he went down the embankment, making his way, first through trees and then through a patch of dead horseweed stalks, to the creek. A little way upstream he came to a place of large flat rocks that had been swept clean by the creek and were now in the sun and dry. Opening the duffel bag, he carefully laid its contents out on the rocks. He took out his razor and brush and soap and a small mirror, and knelt beside the stream and soaped his face and shaved. The water was cold, but he had shaved with cold water before. When he had shaved, he took off his clothes and, standing in flowing water that instantly made his feet ache, he bathed, quaking and breathing between his teeth as he raised the cold water again and again in his cupped hands.

Standing on the rocks in the sun, he dried himself with the shirt he had been wearing. He put on his clean, too-large clothes, tied his tie, and combed his hair. And then warmth came to him. It came from inside himself and from the sun outside; he felt suddenly radiant in every vein and fiber of his body. He was clean and warm and rested and hungry. He was well.

He was in his own country now, and he did not see anything around him that he did not know.

"I have been a stranger and have seen strange things," he thought. "And now I am where it is not strange, and I am not a stranger."

He was sitting on the rocks, resting after his bath. His bag, repacked, lay on the rock beside him and he propped his elbow on it.

"I am not a stranger, but I am changed. Now I know a mighty power that can pass over the earth and make it strange. There are people, where I have been, that won't know their places when they get back to them. Them that live to get back won't be where they were when they left."

He became sleepy and he lay down on the rock and slept. He slept more deeply than he had in the night. He dreamed he was where he was, and a great, warm light fell upon that place, and there was light within it and within him.

When he returned to the road after his bath and his sleep, it was past the middle of the morning. His steps fell into their old rhythm on the blacktop.

"I know a mighty power," he thought. "A mighty power of death and fire. An anger beyond the power of any man, made big in machines equal to many men. And a little man who has passed through mighty death and fire and still lived—what is he going to think of himself when he is back again, walking the river road below Port William, that we would have blowed all to flinders as soon as look at it if it had got in our way?"

He walked, as before, the left side of the road, not meaning to ask for rides. But as on the afternoon before, there was little traffic. He had met two cars going down toward Hargrave and had been passed by only one coming up.

Where the road began to rise toward Port William up on the ridge, a lesser road branched off to the left and ran along the floor of the valley. As Art reached this intersection, he heard a truck engine backfiring, coming down the hill, and then the truck came into sight and he recognized it. It was an old green International driven, as he expected and soon saw, by an old man wearing a trucker's cap and smoking a pipe. The truck was loaded with fat hogs, heading for the packing plant at Jefferson. As he went by, the old man waved to Art and Art waved back.

"Sam Hanks," he thought. "I have been gone over three years and have traveled a many a thousand miles over land and ocean, and in all that time and all them miles the first man I have seen that I have always known is Sam Hanks."

He tried to think what person he had seen last when he was leaving, but he could not remember. He took the lesser road and, after perhaps half a mile, turned into a road still narrower, only a pair of graveled wheel tracks. A little later, when the trees were fully leaved, this would be almost a burrow, tunneling along between the creek and the hillside under the overarching trees, but now the leaves were small and the sun cast the shadows of the branches in a close network onto the gravel.

Soon he was walking below the high-water line. He could see it clearly marked on the slope to his right: a line above which the fallen leaves of the year before were still bright and below which they were darkened by their long steeping in the flood. The slope under the trees was strewn with drift, and here and there a drift log was lodged in the branches high above his head. In the shadow of the flood the spring was late, the buds of the trees just opening, the white flowers of twinleaf and bloodroot just beginning to bloom. It was almost as if he were walking under water, so abrupt and vivid was the difference above and below the line that marked the crest of the flood. But somewhere high in the sunlit branches a redbird sang over and over in a clear, pealing voice, "Even so, even so."

And there was nothing around him that Art did not know. He knew the place in all the successions of the year: from the little blooms that came in the earliest spring to the fallen red leaves of October, from the songs of the nesting birds to the anxious wintering of the little things that left their tracks in snow, from the first furrow to the last load of the harvest.

Where the creek turned away from the road the valley suddenly widened and opened. The road still held up on the hillside among the trees, permitting him to see, through the intervening branches, the broad field that lay across the bottom. He could see that plowing had been started; a long straight-sided strip had been back-furrowed out across the field, from the foot of the slope below the road to the trees that lined the creek bank. And then he saw, going away from him, almost out to the end of the strip, two mule teams with two plow-men walking in furrows behind them. The plowmen's heads were bent to their work, their hands riding easy on the handles of the plows. Some distance behind the second plowman was a little boy, also walking in the furrow and carrying a tin can; from time to time he bent and picked something up from the freshly turned earth and dropped it into the can. Walking behind the boy was a large hound. The first plowman was Art's father, the second his brother Mart. The boy was Art's sister's son, Roy Lee, who had been two years old when Art left and was now five. The hound was probably Old Bawler who made it a part of his business to be always at work. Roy Lee was collecting fishing worms, and Art looked at the creek and saw, in an open place at the top of the bank, three willow poles stuck into the ground, their lines in the water.

The first of the teams reached the end of the plowland, and Art heard his father's voice clear and quiet: "Gee, boys." And then Mart's team finished their furrow, and Mart said, "Gee, Sally." They went around the headland and started back.

Art stood as if still in his absence, as if looking out of his absence at them, who did not know he was there, and he had to shake his head. He had to shake his head twice to persuade himself that he did not hear, from somewhere off in the distance, the heavy footsteps of artillery rounds striding toward them.

He pressed down the barbed wire at the side of the road, straddled over it, and went down through the trees, stopping at the foot of the slope. They came toward him along the edge of the plowland, cutting it two furrows wider. Soon he could hear the soft footfalls of the mules, the trace ends jingling, the creaking of the doubletrees. Present to himself, still absent to them, he watched them come.

At the end of the furrow his father called, "Gee!" and leaned his plow over so that it could ride around the headland on the share and right handle. And then he saw Art. "Well now!" he said, as if only to himself. "Whoa!" he said to the mules. And again: "Well now!" He came over to Art and put out his hand and Art gave him his.

Art saw that there were tears in his father's eyes, and he grinned and said, "Howdy."

Early Rowanberry stepped back and looked at his son and said again, "Well now!"

Mart came around onto the headland then and stopped his team. He and Art shook hands, grinning at each other.

"You reckon your foot'll still fit in a furrow?"

Art nodded. "I reckon it still will."

"Well, here's somebody you don't hardly know," Mart said, gesturing toward Roy Lee, "and who don't know you at all, I'll bet. Do you know who this fellow is, Roy Lee?"

Roy Lee probably did not know, though he knew he had an uncle who was a soldier. He knew about soldiers—he knew they fought in a war far away—and here was a great, tall, fine soldier in a soldier suit with shining buttons, and the shoes on his feet were shining. Roy Lee felt something akin to awe and something akin to love and something akin to fear. He could not have been more cleanly removed from ordinary life if tongs had reached down from the sky and lifted him into another world. He shook his head and looked down at his bare right foot.

Mart laughed. "This here's your Uncle Art. You know about Uncle Art." To Art he said, "He's talked enough about you. He's been looking out the road to see if you was coming."

Art looked up the creek and across it at the house and outbuildings and barn. He looked at the half-plowed field on the valley floor with the wooded hillsides around it and the blinding blue sky over it. He looked again and again at his father and his young nephew and his brother. They stood up in their lives around him now in such a way that he could not imagine their deaths.

Early Rowanberry looked at his son, now and then

reaching out to grasp his shoulder or his arm, as if to feel through the cloth of the uniform the flesh and bone of the man inside. "Well now!" he said again, and again, "Well now!"

Art reached down and picked up a handful of earth from the furrow nearest him. "You're plowing it just a little wet, ain't you?"

"Well, we've had a wet time," Mart said. "We felt like we had to go ahead. Maybe we'll get another hard frost. We could yet."

Art said, "Well, I reckon we might."

And then he heard his father's voice riding up in his throat as he had never heard it, and he saw that his father had turned to the boy and was speaking to him:

"Honey, run yonder to the house. Tell your granny to set on another plate. For we have our own that was gone and has come again."

4

Fidelity

Lyda had not slept, and she knew that Danny had not either. It was close to midnight. They had turned out the light two hours earlier, and since then they had lain side by side, not moving, not touching, disturbed beyond the power to think by the thought of the old man who was lying slack and still in the mechanical room, in the merciless light, with a tube in his nose and a tube needled into his arm and a tube draining his bladder into a plastic bag that hung beneath the bed. The old man had not answered to his name, "Uncle Burley." He did not, in fact, appear to belong to his name at all, for his eyes were shut, he breathed with the help of a machine, and an unearthly pallor shone on his forehead and temples. His hands did not move. From time to time, unable to look any longer at him or at the strange, resistant objects around him in the room, they looked at each other, and their eyes met in confusion, as if they had come to the wrong place.

They had gone after supper to the hospital in Louisville to enact again the strange rite of offering themselves where they could not be received. They were brought back as if by mere habit into the presence of a life that had once included them and now did not, for it was a life that, so far as they could see, no longer included even itself. And so they stood around the image on the bed and waited for whatever completion would let them go.

There were four of them: Nathan Coulter, Burley's nephew, who might as well have been his son; Danny Branch, his son in fact, who had until recent years passed more or less as his nephew and who called him "Uncle Burley" like the others; and there were Nathan's wife, Hannah, and Lyda, Danny's wife, who might as well have been his daughters.

After a while, Hannah rested her purse on the bed, and opened it, and took out a handkerchief with which she touched the corners of her eyes. She put the handkerchief back into her purse and slowly shut the clasp, watching her hands with care as if she were sewing. And then she looked up at Nathan with a look that acknowledged everything, and Nathan turned and went out, and the others followed.

.　　　.　　　.

All through the latter part of the summer Burley had been, as he said himself, "as no-account as a cut cat." But he had stayed with them, helping as he could, through the tobacco harvest, and they were glad to have him with them, to listen to his stories, and to work around him when he got in their way. He had begun to lose the use of himself, his body only falteringly answerable to his will. He blamed it on arthritis. "There's a whole family of them Ritis boys," he would say, "and that Arthur's the meanest one of the bunch." But the problem was not arthritis. Burley was only saying what he knew that other old men had said before him; he was too inexperienced in illness himself to guess what might be wrong with him.

They had a fence to build before corn gathering, and they kept him with them at that. "We'll need you to line the posts," they told him. But by then they could not keep him awake. They would find him asleep wherever they left him, in his chair at home, or in the cab of a pickup, or hunched in his old hunting coat against an end post or the trunk of a tree. One day, laying a hand on Burley's shoulder to wake him, Danny felt what his eyes had already told him but what he had forborne to know with his hand: that where muscle had once piled and rounded under the cloth, there was now little more than hide and bone.

"We've got to do something for him," Danny said then, partly because Lyda had been saying it insistently to him.

Nathan stared straight at him as only Nathan could do. "What?"

"Take him to the doctor, I reckon. He's going to die."

"Damn right. He's eighty-two years old, and he's sick."

They were getting ready to go in to dinner, facing each other across the bed of Danny's pickup where they had come to put their tools. Burley, who had not responded to the gentle shake that Danny had given him, was still asleep in the cab.

Nathan lifted over the side of the truck a bucket containing staples and pliers and a hammer, and then, as he would not ordinarily have done, he pitched in his axe. "He's never been to a doctor since I've known him. He said he wouldn't go. You going to knock him in the head before you take him?"

"We'll just take him."

Nathan stood a moment with his head down. When he looked up again, he said, "Well."

So they took him. They took him because they wanted to do more for him than they could do, and they could think of nothing else. Nathan held out the longest, and he gave in only because he was uncertain.

"Are you—are we—just going to let him die like an old animal?" Hannah asked.

And Nathan, resistant and grouchy in his discomfort, said, "An old animal is maybe what he wants to die like."

"But don't we need to help him?"

"Yes. And we don't know what to do, and we're not going to know until after we've done it. Whatever it is. What better can we wish him than to die in his sleep out at work with us or under a tree somewhere?"

"Oh," Hannah said, "if only he already had!"

Nathan and Danny took him to the doctor in Nathan's pickup, Nathan's being more presentable and dependable than Danny's, which anyhow had their fencing tools in it. The doctor pronounced Burley "a very sick man"; he wanted him admitted to the hospital. And so, the doctor having called ahead, with Burley asleep between them Danny and Nathan took him on to Louisville, submitted to the long interrogation required for admission, saw him undressed and gowned and put to bed by a jolly nurse, and left him. As they were going out, he said, "Boys, why don't you all wait for me yonder by the gate. I've got just this one last round to make, and then we'll all go in together." They did not know from what field or what year he was talking.

Burley was too weak for surgery, the doctor told them the next day. It would be necessary to build up his strength. In the meantime tests would be performed. Danny and Lyda, Nathan and Hannah stood with the doctor in the corridor outside Burley's room. The doctor held his glasses in one hand and a clipboard in the other. "We hope to have him on his feet again very soon," he said.

And that day, when he was awake, Burley was plainly disoriented and talking out of his head—"saying some things," as Nathan later told Wheeler Catlett, "that he never thought of before and some that nobody ever thought of before." He was no longer in his right mind, they thought, because he was no longer in his right place. When they could bring him home again, he would be himself.

Those who loved him came to see him: Hannah and Nathan, Lyda and Danny, Jack Penn, Andy and Flora Catlett, Arthur and Martin Rowanberry, Wheeler and his other son and law partner, Henry, and their wives. They sat or stood around Burley's bed, reconstructing their membership around him in that place that hummed, in the lapses of their talk, with the sounds of many engines. Burley knew them all, was pleased to have them there with him, and appeared to understand where he was and what was happening. But in the course of his talk with them, he spoke also to their dead, whom he seemed to see standing with them. Or he would raise his hand and ask them to listen to the hounds that had been running day and night in the bottom on the other side of the river. Once he said, "It's right outlandish what we've got started in this country, big political vats and tubs on every roost."

And then, in the midst of the building of strength and the testing, Burley slipped away toward death. But the people of the hospital did not call it dying; they called it a coma. They spoke of curing him. They spoke of his recovery.

A coma, the doctor explained, was certainly not beyond expectation. It was not hopeless, he said. They must wait and see.

And they said little in reply, for what he knew was not what they knew, and his hope was not theirs.

"Well, then," Nathan said to the doctor, "we'll wait and see."

Burley remained attached to the devices of breathing and feeding and voiding, and he did not wake up. The doctor stood before them again, explaining confidently and with many large words, that Mr. Coulter soon would be well, that there were yet other measures that could be taken, that they should not give up hope, that there were places well-equipped to care for patients in Mr. Coulter's condition, that they should not worry. And then he said that if he and his colleagues could not help Mr. Coulter, they could at least make him comfortable. He spoke fluently from within the bright orderly enclosure of his explanation, like a man in a glass booth. And Nathan and Hannah, Danny and Lyda stood looking in at him from the larger, looser, darker order of their merely human love.

When they returned on yet another visit and found the old body still as it had been, a mere passive addition to the complicated machines that kept it minimally alive, they saw finally that in their attempt to help they had not helped but only complicated his disease beyond their power to help. And they thought with regret of the time when the thing that was wrong with him had been simply unknown, and there had been only it and him and him and them in the place they had known together. Loving him, wanting to help him, they had given him over to "the best of modern medical care"—which meant, as they now saw, that they had abandoned him.

If Lyda was wakeful, then, it was because she, like the others, was shaken by the remorse of a kind of treason.

.   .   .

Lyda must have dozed finally, because she did not hear Danny get up. When she opened her eyes, the light was on, and he was standing at the foot of the bed, buttoning his shirt. The clock on the dresser said a quarter after twelve.

"What are you doing?"

"Go back to sleep, Lyda. I'm going to get him."

She did not ask who. She said "Good," which made him look at her, but he did not say more.

And she did not ask. He suited her, and moreover she was used to him. He was the kind, and it was not a strange kind to her, who might leave the bed in the middle of the night if he heard his hounds treed somewhere and not come back for hours. Like Burley, Danny belonged half to the woods. Lyda knew this and it did not disturb her, for he also belonged to her, in the woods as at home.

He finished dressing, turned the light off, and went out. She heard him in Burley's room and then in the kitchen. She heard the scrape of the latchpin at the smoke-house door. He was being quiet; she would not have heard him if she had not listened carefully. But then the hounds complained aloud when he shut them in a stall in the barn.

Presently he came back, and she seemed to feel rather than hear or see him as he moved into the doorway and stopped. "I don't know how long I'll be gone. You and the kids'll have to do the chores and look after things."

"All right."

"I fastened up the dogs."

"I heard you."

"Well, don't let them out. And listen, Lyda. If somebody wants to know, I've said something about Indiana."

She listened until she heard the old pickup start and go out the lane. And then she slept.

Danny's preparations were swift and scant but sufficient for several days. He stripped the bedclothes from Burley's bed, laid them out neatly on the kitchen floor, and then rolled them up around a slab of cured jowl from the smokehouse, a small iron skillet, and a partly emptied bag of cornmeal. He tied the bundle with baling twine, making a sling by which it could hang from his shoulder. From behind the back hall door he took his hunting coat with his flashlight in one pocket and his old long-barreled .22 pistol in the other. He removed the pistol and laid it on top of the dish cabinet.

His pickup truck was sitting in front of the barn, and the confined hounds wailed again at the sound of his footsteps.

"Hush!" he said, and they hushed.

He pitched his bundle onto the seat and unlatched and raised the hood. He had filled the tank with gas that afternoon but had not checked the oil and water. By both principle and necessity, he had never owned a new motor vehicle in his life. The present pickup was a third-hand Dodge, which Burley had liked to describe as "a loose association of semiretired parts, like me." But Danny was, in self-defense, a good mechanic, and he and the old truck and the box of tools that he always kept on the floorboard made a working unit that mostly worked.

The oil was all right. He poured a little water into the radiator, relatched the hood, set the bucket back on the well-top, and got into the truck. He started the engine, backed around in front of the corncrib, turned on the headlights, headed out the lane—and so committed himself to the succession of ever wider and faster roads that led to the seasonless, sunless, and moonless world where Burley lay in his bonds.

The old truck roaring in outlandish disproportion to its speed, he drove through Port William and down the long slant into the river bottoms where the headlights showed the ripening fields of corn. After a while he slowed and turned left onto the interstate, gaining speed again as he went down the ramp. The traffic on the great road was thinner than in the daytime but constant nevertheless. As he entered the flow of it, he accelerated until the vibrating needle of the speedometer stood at sixty miles an hour—twenty miles faster than he usually drove. If at the crescendo of this acceleration the truck had blown up, it would not altogether have surprised him. Nor would it altogether have displeased him. He hated the interstate and the reeking stream of traffic that poured along it day and night, and he liked the old truck only insofar as it was a salvage job and his own. "If she blows," he thought, "I'll try to stop her crosswise of both lanes."

But though she roared and groaned and panted and complained, she did not blow.

.　　　.　　　.

Danny's mother, Kate Helen Branch, had been the love of Burley Coulter's life. They were careless lovers, those two, and Danny came as a surprise—albeit a far greater surprise to Burley than to Kate Helen. Danny was born to his mother's name, a certified branch of the Branches, and he grew up in the care of his mother and his mother's mother in a small tin-roofed, paper-sided house on an abandoned corner of Thad Spellman's farm, not far from town and even closer, by a shortcut up through the woods, to the Coulter Place. As the sole child in that womanly household, Danny was more than amply mothered. And he did not go fatherless, for Burley was that household's faithful visitor, its pillar and provider. He took a hand in Danny's upbringing from the start, although, since the boy was nominally a Branch, Danny always knew his father as "Uncle Burley."

If Danny became a more domestic man than his father, that is because he loved the frugal, ample household run by his mother and grandmother and later by his mother and himself. He loved his mother's ability to pinch and mend and make things last. He was secretly proud of her small stitches in the patches of his clothes. They kept a big garden and a small flock of hens. They kept a pig in a pen to eat scraps and make meat, and they kept a Jersey cow that picked a living in the green months out of Thad Spellman's thickety pasture. The necessary corn for the pig and chickens and the corn and hay for the cow were provided by Burley and soon enough by Burley and Danny.

If Danny became a better farmer than his father that is because, through Burley, he came under the influence of Burley's brother, Jarrat, and of Jarrat's son, Nathan, and of Burley's and Nathan's friend, Mat Feltner, all of whom were farmers by calling and by devotion. From them he learned the ways that people lived by their soil and their care of it, by the bounty of crops and animals, and by the power of horses and mules.

But if Danny became more a man of the woods and the streams than nearly anybody else of his place and time, that was because of Burley himself. For Burley was by calling and by devotion a man of the woods and streams. When duty did not keep him in the fields, he would be hunting or fishing or roaming about in search of herbs or wild fruit, or merely roaming about to see what he could see; and from the time Danny was old enough to want to go along, Burley took him. He taught him to be quiet and watch and not complain, to hunt, to trap, to fish and swim. He taught him the names of the trees and of all the wild plants of the woods. Danny's first providings on his own to his mother's household were of wild goods: fish and game, nuts and berries that grew by no human effort but furnished themselves to him in response only to his growing intimacy with the countryside. Such providing pleased him and made him proud. Soon he augmented it with wages and produce from the farmwork he did with Burley and the others.

The world that Danny was born into during the tobacco harvest of 1932 suited him well. That the nation was poor was hardly noticeable to him, whose people had never been rich except in the things that they continued to be rich in though they were poor. He loved his half-wooded native country of ridge and hillside and hollow and creek and river bottom. And he loved the horse- and mule-powered independent farming of that place and time.

When Danny had finished the eighth grade at the Port William school, he was growing a crop of his own and was nearly as big as he was going to get, a little taller and a good deal broader than his father. He was a trapper of mink and muskrat, a hunter and fisherman. He farmed for himself or for wages every day that he was out of school and in the mornings and evenings before and after school. If Burley had not continued to be Kate Helen's main provider, Danny could and would have been.

When he began to ride the bus to the high school at Hargrave, the coaches, gathering around him and feeling his arms and shoulders admiringly as if he had been a horse, invited him to go out for basketball. He gave them the smile, direct and a little merry, by which he reserved himself to himself, and said, "I reckon I already got about all I can do."

He quit school the day he was sixteen and never thought of it again. By then he was growing a bigger crop, and he owned a good team of mules, enough tools of his own to do his work, and two hounds. When he married Lyda two years later, he had, except for a farm of his own, everything he had thought of to want.

By then the old way of farming was coming to an end. But Danny never gave it up.

"Don't you reckon you ought to go ahead and get you a tractor, like everybody else?" Burley asked him.

And Danny looked up at him from the hoof of the mule he was at that moment shoeing and smiled his merry smile. "I ain't a-going to pay a company," he said, "to go and get what is already here."

"Well," Burley said, though he knew far better than the Hargrave basketball coach the meaning of that smile, "tractors don't eat when they ain't working."

Danny drove in a nail, bent over the point, and reached for another nail. He did not look up this time when he spoke, and it was the last he would say on the matter: "They don't eat *grass* when they ain't working."

That was as much as Burley had wanted to say. He liked mules better than tractors himself and had only gone along with the change to accommodate his brother, Jarrat, who, tireless himself, wanted something to work that did not get tired.

Burley loved to be in the woods with the hounds at night, and Danny inherited that love early and fully. They hunted sometimes with their neighbors, Arthur and Martin Rowanberry, sometimes with Elton Penn, but as often as not there would be just the two of them—man and little boy, and then man and big boy, and at last two men—out together in the dark-mystified woods of the hollows and slopes and bottomlands, hunting sometimes all night, but enacting too their general approval of the weather and the world. Sometimes, when the hunting was slow, they would stop in a sheltered place and build a fire. Sometimes, while their fire burned and the stars or the clouds moved slowly over them, they lay down and slept.

There was another kind of hunting that Burley did

alone. Danny did not know of this until after Kate Helen died, when he and Lyda got married and, at Burley's invitation, moved into the old weatherboarded log house on the Coulter home place where Burley had lived alone for fourteen years. There were times—though never when he was needed at work—when Burley just disappeared, and Danny and Lyda would know where he had gone only because the hounds would disappear at the same time. Little by little, Danny came to understand.

In love Burley had assumed many responsibilities. In love and responsibility, as everyone must, he had acquired his griefs and losses, guilts and sorrows. Sometimes, under the burden of these, he sought the freedom of solitude in the woods. He might be gone for two or three days or more, living off the land and whatever leftovers of biscuits or cornbread he might be carrying in his pockets, sleeping in barns or in the open by the side of a fire. If the dogs became baffled and gave up or went home, Burley went on, walking slowly hour after hour along the steep rims of the valleys where the trees were old. When he returned, he would be smiling, at ease and quiet, as if his mind just fit within his body.

"Don't quit," Danny said to the truck, joking with it as he sometimes did with his children or his animals. "It's going to be downhill all the way home."

He was making an uproar, and uproar gathered around him as he came to the outskirts of the city. The trailer trucks, sleek automobiles, and other competent vehicles now pressing around him made him aware of the disproportion between his shuddering, smoking old pickup and the job he had put it to, and he began to grin. He came to his exit and roared down into the grid of streets and lights. He continued to drive aggressively. Though he had no plan to speak of, it yet seemed to him that what he had to do required him to keep up a good deal of momentum.

At the hospital, he drove to the emergency entrance, parked as close to the door as he could without being too much in the light, got out, and walked to the door as a man walks who knows exactly what he is doing and is already a little late. His cap, which usually sat well to the back of his head, he had now pulled forward until the bill was nearly parallel with his nose. Only when he was out of the truck and felt the air around him again, did he realize that it was making up to rain.

The emergency rooms and corridors were filled with the bloodied and the bewildered, for it was now the tail end of another Friday night of the Great American Spare-Time Civil War. Danny walked through the carnage like a man who was used to it.

Past a set of propped-open double doors, an empty gurney was standing against the corridor wall, its sheets neatly folded upon it. Without breaking stride, he took hold of it and went rapidly on down the corridor, pushing the gurney ahead of him. When he came to an elevator, he thumbed the "up" button and waited.

When the doors opened, he saw that a small young nurse was already in the elevator, standing beside the control panel. He pushed the gurney carefully past her, nodding to her and smiling. He said, "Four, please."

She pushed the button. The doors closed. She looked at him, sighed, and shook her head. "It's been a long night."

"Well," he said, "it ain't as long as it has been."

At the fourth floor the doors slid open. He pushed the gurney off the elevator.

"Good night," the nurse said.

He said, "Good night."

He had to go by the fourth floor nurse's station, but there was only one nurse there and she was talking with vehemence into the telephone. She did not look up.

The door of Burley's room was shut. Danny pushed the gurney in and reshut the door. Now he was frightened, and yet there was no caution in him; he did not give himself time to think or to hesitate. Burley was lying white and still in the pallid light. Danny took a pair of rubber gloves from the container affixed to the wall and put them on. Wetting a rag at the wash basin, he carefully washed the handle of the gurney. He then pushed the gurney up near the bed and removed the folded sheet from it. Leaning over the bed, he spoke in a low voice to Burley. "Listen. I'm going to take you home. Don't worry. It's me. It's Danny."

Gently he withdrew the tube from Burley's nose. Gently he pulled away the adhesive tapes and took the needle out of Burley's arm. He took hold of the tube of the bladder catheter as if to pull it out also and then, thinking again, took out his pocketknife and cut the tube in two.

He gathered Burley into his arms and held him a moment, surprised by his lightness, and then gently he laid him onto the gurney. He unfolded the sheet and draped it over Burley, covering him entirely from head to foot. He opened the door, pushed the gurney through, and closed the door.

The nurse at the nurse's station was still on the phone. "I told you no," she was saying. "N, O, period. You have just got to understand, when I say no, I *mean* no."

Near the elevator two janitors were leaning against the wall, mops in hand, as stupefied, apparently, as the soldiers at the Tomb.

When the elevator arrived, the same nurse was on it. She gave him a smile of recognition. "My goodness, I believe we must be on the same schedule tonight."

"Yes, mam," he said.

She hardly glanced at the still figure on the gurney. "She's used to it," he thought. But he was careful, nonetheless, to stand in such a way as to make it hard for her to see, if she looked, that this corpse was breathing.

"One?" she asked.

"Yes, mam," he said. "If you please."

Once out of the elevator, he rolled the gurney rapidly down the corridor and through the place of emergency.

A man with a bandaged eye stood aside as Danny approached and went without stopping out through the automatic doors.

A slow rain had begun to fall, and now the pavement was shining.

The Coulter Lane turned off the blacktop a mile or so beyond Port William. Danny drove past the lane, following the blacktop on down again into the river valley. Presently he turned left onto a gravel road, and after a mile or so turned left again into the lower end of the Coulter Lane, passable now for not much more than a hundred yards. Where a deep gulley had been washed across the road, he stopped the truck. He was in a kind of burrow, deep under the trees in a narrow crease of the hill: the Stepstone Hollow.

He switched off the engine and sat still, letting the quiet and the good darkness settle around him. He had been gone perhaps two hours and a half, and not for a minute during that time had he ceased to hurry. So resolutely had he kept up the momentum of his haste that his going and his coming back had been as much one movement as a leap. And now, that movement completed, he began to take his time. In the quiet he could hear Burley's breathing, slow and shallow but still regular. He heard, too, the slow rain falling on the woods and the trees dripping steadily onto the roof of the truck. "Well," he said quietly to Burley, "here's somewhere you've been before."

The shallow breathing merely continued out of the dark where Burley, wrapped in his sheet, slumped against the door.

"Listen," Danny said. "We're in the Stepstone Hollow. It's raining just a little drizzling rain, and the trees are dripping. That's what you hear. You can pret' near just listen and tell where you are. In a minute I'm going to take you up to the old barn. You don't have a thing to worry about anymore."

He got out and stood a moment, accepting the dark

and the rain. There was, in spite of the overcast, some brightness in the sky. He could see a little. He took his flashlight from the pocket of his coat and blinked it once. The bundle of bedclothes and food that he had brought from the house lay with the coat on the seat beside Burley. Danny dragged the bundle out and suspended it from his right shoulder, shortening the string to make the load as manageable as possible. Taking the flashlight, he then went around the truck and gently opened the door on the other side. He tucked the sheet snugly around Burley and then covered his head and chest with the coat.

"Now," he said, "I'm going to pick you up and carry you a ways."

Keeping the flashlight in his right hand, he gathered Burley up into his arms, kneed the door shut, and started up the hollow through the rain. He used the light to cross the gulley. Beyond there, he needed only to blink the light occasionally to show himself the lay of things. Though his burden was awkward and the wet and drooping foliage brushed him on both sides, he could walk without trouble. He made almost no sound and was grateful for the silence and slowness and effort after his loud passage out from the city. It occurred to him then that this was a season-changing rain. Tomorrow would be clear and cool, the first fall day.

It was a quarter of a mile or more up to the barn, and his arms were aching well before he got there, but having once taken this burden up, he dared not set it down. The barn, doorless and sagging, stood on a tiny shelf of bottomland beside the branch. It was built in the young manhood of Dave Coulter, Burley's father, to house the tobacco crops from the fields, now long abandoned and overgrown, on the north slopes above it. Abandoned along with its fields, the barn had been used for many years only by groundhogs and other wild creatures and by Burley and Danny, who had sheltered there on rainy days and nights. Danny knew this place in the dark as well as if he could see it. On the old northward-facing slopes on one side of the branch was a thicket of forty-year-old trees: redbud, elm, box elder, walnut, locust, ash—the trees of the "pioneer generation," returning the fields to the forest. On the south slope, where the soil was rockier and shallower, stood the uninterrupted forest of white and red oaks and chinquapins, hickories, ashes, and maples, many of them two or three hundred years old.

Needing the light now that they were in the cavern of the barn, Danny carried Burley the length of the drive-way, stepping around a derelict wagon and then into a stripping room attached at one corner. This was a small shed that was tighter and better preserved than the barn. A bench ran the length of the north side under a row of windows. Danny propped Burley against the wall at the near end of the bench, which he then swept clean with an old burlap sack. He made a pallet of the bedclothes and laid Burley on it and covered him.

"Now," he said, "I've got to go back to the truck for some things. You're in the old barn on Stepstone, and you're all right. I won't be gone but a few minutes."

He shone the light a moment on the still face. In its profound sleep, it wore a solemnity that Burley, in his waking life, would never have allowed. And yet it was, as it had not been in the hospital, unmistakably the face of the man who for eighty-two years had been Burley Coulter. Here, where it belonged, the face thus identified itself and assumed a power that kept Danny standing there, shining the light on it, and that made him say to himself with care, "Now these are the last things. Now what happens will not happen again in his life."

He hurried back along the road to the truck and removed an axe, a spade, and a heavy steel spud bar from among the fencing tools in the back. The rain continued, falling steadily as it had fallen since it began. He shouldered the bar and spade and, carrying the axe in his left hand, returned to the barn.

Burley had not moved. He breathed on, as steadily and forcelessly as the falling rain.

"You're in a good place," Danny said. "You've slept here before and you're all right. Now I've got to sleep a little myself. I'll be close by."

He was tired at last. There were several sheets of old roofing stacked in the barn, and he took two of these, laying one on the floor just inside the open door nearest to the shed where Burley slept and propping the other as a shield from the draft that was pulling up the driveway. He lay down on his back and folded his arms on his chest. His clothes were damp, but with his hunting coat snug around him he was warm enough.

Though in his coming and going he had hardly made a sound, once he lay still the woods around the barn reassembled a quiet that was larger and older than his own. It was as though the woods had stopped whatever it was doing to regard him as he entered, had permitted itself to be distracted by him and his burden and his task, and now that he had ceased to move it went back to its unfinished preoccupations. The rain went on with its steady patter on the barn roof and on the leafy woods.

Danny lay still and thought of all that had happened since nightfall and of what he might yet have ahead of him. For a while he continued to feel in all his nerves the swaying of the old truck as it sped along the curves of the highway. And then he ceased to think either of the past or of what was to come. The rain continued to fall. The flowing branch made a varying little song in his mind. His mind went slowly to and fro with a dark treetop in the wind. And then he slept.

Lyda had the telephone put in when they closed the school in Port William and began to haul even the littlest children all the way to the consolidated grade school at Hargrave. This required a bus ride of an hour and a half each way for the Branch children and took them much farther out of reach than they had ever been.

"They'll be gone from before daylight to after dark in the winter, who with we don't know, doing what we don't know," Lyda said, "and they've *got* to be able to call home if they need to."

"All right," Danny said. "And there won't anybody call us up on it but the kids—is that right?"

When it rang at night, it just scared Lyda to death, even when the kids were home. If Danny was gone, she always started worrying about him when she heard the phone ring.

She hurried down to the kitchen in her nightgown. She made a swipe at the light switch beside the kitchen door, but missed and went ahead anyhow. There was no trouble in finding the telephone in the dark; it went right on ringing as if she weren't rushing to answer it.

"Hello?" she said.

"Hello. May I speak to Mr. Daniel Branch, please?" It was a woman's voice, precise and correct.

"Danny's not here. I'm his wife. Can I help you?"

"Can you tell us how to get in touch with Mr. Branch?"

"No. He said something about Indiana, but I don't know where."

There was a pause, as though the voice at the other end were preparing itself.

"Mrs. Branch, this is the hospital. I'm afraid I have some very disturbing news. Mr. Coulter—Mr. Burley Coulter—has disappeared."

"Oh!" Lyda said. She was grinning into the dark, and there had been a tremor of relief in her voice that she trusted might have passed for dismay.

"Oh, my goodness!" she said finally.

"Let me assure you, Mrs. Branch, that the entire hospital staff is deeply concerned about this. We have, of course, notified the police—"

"Oh!" Lyda said.

"—and all other necessary steps will be taken. Please have your husband contact us as soon as he returns."

"I will," Lyda said.

After she hung up, Lyda stood thinking in the dark a moment. And then she turned on the light and called Henry Catlett, whose phone rang a long time before he answered. She was not sure yet that she needed a lawyer, but she could call Henry as a friend.

"Henry, it's Lyda. I'm sorry to get you up in the middle of the night."

"It's all right," Henry said.

"The hospital just called. Uncle Burley has disappeared."

"Disappeared?"

"That's what the lady said."

There was a pause.

"Where's Danny?"

"He's gone."

"I see."

There was another pause.

"Did he say where he was going?"

"He said something about Indiana, Henry. That's all he said."

"He said that, and that's all?"

"About."

"Did you tell that to the lady from the hospital?"

"Yes."

"Did she want to know anything else?"

"No."

"And you didn't tell her anything else?"

"No."

"Did *she* say anything else?"

"She said the police had been notified."

There was another pause.

"What time is it, Lyda?"

"Three o'clock. A little after."

"And you and the kids will have the morning chores

to do, and you'll have to get the kids fed and off to school."

"That's right."

"So you'll have to be there for a while. Maybe that's all right. But you'll have to expect a call or maybe a visit from the police, Lyda. When you talk to them, tell them exactly what you told the lady at the hospital. Tell the truth, but don't tell any more than you've already told. If they want to know more, tell them I'm your lawyer and they must talk to me."

"I will."

"Are you worried about Burley and Danny?"

"No."

"Are you worried about talking to the police?"

"I'm uneasy, but I'm not worried."

"All right. Let's try to sleep some more. Tomorrow might be a busy day."

Danny woke cold and hungry. He was lying on his back with his arms folded on his chest; he had slept perhaps two hours, and he had not moved. Nor had anything moved in the barn or in the wooded hollow around it, so far as he could tell, except the little stream of Stepstone, which continued to make the same steady song it had been making when he fell asleep. A few crickets sang. The air was still, and in openings of mist that had gathered in the hollow he could see the stars.

Though he was cold, for several minutes he did not move. He loved the stillness and was reluctant to break it. An owl trilled nearby and another answered some distance away. Danny turned onto his side to face the opening of the doorway, pillowed his head on his left forearm, and, taking off his cap, ran the fingers of his right hand slowly through his hair.

He yawned, stretched, and got up. Taking the flashlight, he went in to where Burley lay and shone the light on him. Nothing had changed. The old body breathed on with the same steady yet forceless and shallow breaths. Danny saw at once all he needed to see, and yet he remained for a few moments, shining the light. And he said again in his mind, "These are the last things now. Everything that happens now happens for the last time in his life." He reached out with his hand and took hold of Burley's shoulder and shook it gently, as if to waken him, but he did not wake.

"It'll soon be morning," he said aloud. "I'm hungry now. I need to make a fire and fix a little breakfast before the light comes. We can't send up any smoke after daylight. I'll be close by."

He gathered dry scraps of wood from the barn floor, and then he pried loose a locust tierpole with the bark still on it and rapidly cut it into lengths with the axe. Just outside the doorway, he made a small fire between two rocks on which he set his skillet. By the light of the flashlight he sliced a dozen thick slices from the jowl and started several of them frying. He crossed the creek to where a walled spring flowed out of the hillside. He found the rusted coffee can that he kept there, dipped it full and drank, and then dipped it full again. Carrying the filled can, he went back to his fire, where he knelt on one knee and attended to the skillet. The birds had begun to sing, and the sky was turning pale above the eastward trees.

When all the meat was fried, he set the skillet off the fire. With water from the spring and grease from the fried meat, he moistened some cornmeal and made six hoecakes, each the size of the skillet. When he was finished with his cooking, he took the pair of surgical gloves from his pocket and stirred them in the fire until they were burned. He brought water from the creek then and put out the fire. He divided the food carefully and ate half of it. He ate slowly and with pleasure, watching the light come. Movement, fire, and now the food in his belly had taken the chill out of his flesh, but fall was in the air that morning, and he welcomed it. The day would be clear and fine. And more would come—brisk, bright, dark-shadowed days colored by the turning leaves, days that would call up the hunter feeling in him. Suddenly he remembered Elton Penn walking into the woods under the stars of a bright frosty night, half singing, as his way was, "Clear as a bell, cold as hell, and smells like old cheese." Now Elton was three years dead.

As Danny watched, the light reddened and warmed in the sky. The last of the stars disappeared. Above him, on both sides of the hollow, the wet leaves of the treetops began to shine among the fading strands and shelves of mist. Eastward, the mist took a stain of pink from the rising sun and glowed. And Danny felt a happiness that he knew was not his at all, that did not exist because he felt it but because it was here and he had returned to it.

He carried his skillet to the creek, scoured it out with handfuls of a fine gravel that he found there and left it on a rock to dry.

He picked his way through the young thicket growth closing around the barn and entered the stand of old trees that covered the south slope. There the great trees stood around him, the thready night mists caught in their branches, and every leaf was still. When the first white man in this place—the first Coulter or Catlett or Feltner or whoever it was—had passed through this crease of the hill, these trees were here, and the stillness in which they stood and grew had been here forever.

Timber cutters, in recent years, had had their eye on these trees and had approached Burley about "harvesting" them. "I reckon you had better talk to Danny here," Burley said. And Danny smiled that completely friendly, totally impenetrable smile of his, and merely shook his head.

Now Danny was looking for a place well in among the big trees and yet not too far from the creek or too readily accessible to the eye. His study took him a while, but finally he saw what he was looking for. Under a tall, straight chinquapin that was sound and not too old, a tree that would be standing a long time, there was a shallow trough in the ground, left perhaps by the uprooting of another tree a long time ago; the place was open and clear of undergrowth but could not be seen except against a patch of thicket around a windfall. Danny stood and thought again to test his satisfaction, and was satisfied.

As he turned away he noticed, strung between two saplings, the dew-beaded orb of a large orange spider. He stopped to look at it and soon found the spider's home, a sort of tube fashioned of two leaves and so not easy to see, where the spider could withdraw to sleep or take shelter from the rain. It would not be long, Danny thought, before the spiders would have to go out of business for the winter. Soon there would be hard frosts, and the webs would be cumbered and torn by the falling leaves.

Sunlight now filled the sky above the shadowy woods. He went back to the barn, preoccupied with his thoughts, and so he was startled, on entering the stripping room, by Burley's opened eyes, looking at him.

He stopped, for the force of his surprise was almost that of fright. And then he went over to the bench and laid his hand on Burley's. Burley's eyes were perfectly calm; he was smiling. Slowly, pausing to breathe between phrases, he said, "I allowed you'd get here about the same time I did."

"Well, you were right," Danny said. "We made it. Do you know where you are?"

Again, smiling, Burley spoke, his voice so halting and weak as to seem not uttered by bodily strength at all but by some pure presence of recollection and will: "Right here."

He was quoting himself as the hero of an old joke and an old story in which, lost on a night hunt, his companions had asked him where they were, and he had told them, "Right here."

"You're right again," Danny said, knowing that Burley did know where he was. "Are you comfortable? Is there anything you want?"

This time Burley only said, "Drink." He turned his

head a little and looked at the treetops beyond the window.

Danny said, "I'll go to the spring."

At the spring, he drank and then dipped up a drink for Burley. When he returned, Burley's eyes were closed again, and he looked more deeply sunk within himself than before. It was as though his soul, like a circling hawk, had swung back into this world on a wide curve, to look once more out of his eyes at what he had always known and to speak with his voice, and then had swung out of it again, the curve widening. Danny stood still, holding the can of water. He could hear Burley's breaths coming slower than before, tentative and unsteady. Danny listened. He picked up Burley's wrist and held it. And then he shouldered his tools and went up into the woods and began to dig.

Henry Catlett tried hard to take his own advice, but one thought ran on to another and he could not sleep. There was too much he needed to know that he did not know. Within twenty minutes he saw that he was not going to sleep again. He got up in the dark and, taking care not to disturb Sarah who had gone back to sleep after the phone rang, went downstairs, turned on a light and called the hospital. After some trial and error, he was transferred to the supervisor who had talked to Lyda.

"This is Henry Catlett. I have a little law practice up the river here at Hargrave. I hear you've mislaid one of your patients."

The voice in the receiver became extremely business-like: "The patient would be—?"

"Coulter. Burley Coulter."

"Yes. Well, as you no doubt have heard, Mr. Catlett, Mr. Coulter was reported missing from his room at a little before two o'clock this morning. Such a thing has never happened here before, Mr. Catlett. Let me assure you, sir, that we're doing everything possible on behalf of the victim and his family."

"Of course," Henry said. "I can imagine. Well, I'm calling on behalf of the family. Have you any clues as to what happened?"

"Um. For that, I think I had better have you talk with the investigating officer who was here from the police. Let me find his number. Please hold one minute."

"Take two," Henry said.

She gave him a name and a number, which Henry proceeded to dial.

"Officer Bush," he said, "I'm Henry Catlett, a country lawyer of sorts up at Hargrave. I'm calling on behalf of the family of Mr. Burley Coulter, who seems to have disappeared from his hospital room."

"Yes, Mr. Catlett."

"I understand that you were the investigating officer. What did you find out?"

"Not much, I'm afraid, sir. Mr. Coulter was definitely kidnapped. His attacker disconnected him from the life-support system and wheeled him out, we assume, by way of the emergency entrance. We have one witness, a nurse, who may have seen the kidnapper. She described him as a huge man in a blue shirt; she didn't get a good look at his face. She saw him on an elevator, going up with an empty gurney and down with what she took to be a corpse. Aside from that, we have only the coincidental disappearance of the victim's next of kin, Danny Branch, who his wife says may have gone to Indiana."

"Anything solid? Any fingerprints?"

"Nothing, Mr. Catlett. The man smeared everything he touched, and he didn't touch more than he had to. He may have used a pair of surgical gloves from the room."

"Would you let me know as soon as you have anything more to report?"

"Be glad to."

Henry gave him his phone numbers at home and at the office, thanked him, and hung up. He turned the light off then, felt his way to his easy chair, and sat down in the dark to think.

He knew several things. For one, he knew that Danny Branch, though by no means a small man, would not be described by most people as "huge." So far as he could see at present, all they had to worry about was the blue shirt, and that might be plenty.

He sat thinking until the shapes of the trees outside the window emerged into the first daylight, and then he went back to the phone and called Lyda.

Lyda called Nathan after she had talked to Henry the second time. Nathan, as was his way, said "Hello" and then simply listened. When she had told him of Burley's disappearance and of Danny's, Nathan said, "All right. Do you need anything?"

"No. We'll be fine," she said. "But listen. Henry called back while ago. He said the police didn't find any fingerprints at the hospital. The only witness they found was somebody who saw a man in a blue shirt. Henry wants you and Hannah and me to come to his office as soon as we get our chores done and all. When the police find us, he said, he'd just as soon they'd find us there. He said to tell you, and he'd call Jack and Andy and Flora and the Rowanberrys. He wants everybody who's closest to Burley to be there."

"All right," Nathan said. "It'll be a little while."

He hung up, and having told Lyda's message to Hannah, he put one of his shirts into a paper sack and went out. He had his chores to do, but he would do them later. He got into his pickup and drove out to the Coulter Lane and turned, and turned again into the farm that had been his father's and was now his, divided by a steep, wooded hollow from Burley's place, where Danny and Lyda and their children had lived with Burley since Danny's mother's death. Beyond the two houses in the dawn light, he could see the morning cloud of fog shining in the river valley.

He pulled the truck in behind the house, got out, and started down the hill. Soon he was out of sight among the trees, and he went level along the slope around the point beyond Burley's house, turning gradually out of the river valley into the smaller valley of the creek. He went straight down the hill then to the creek road, turned into the lower end of the Coulter Lane, and soon came to Danny's truck. He saw that Danny's axe and the digging tools were gone.

For several minutes he stood beside the truck, looking up the hollow toward the old barn. And then he took the switch key from where Danny always hid it under a loose flap of floor mat, started the truck and eased it backward along its incoming tracks until it stood on the gravel of the county road. There were a few bald patches of fresh mud that he had had to drive over, and he walked back to these and tramped out the tire tracks, taking care to leave no shoe track of his own.

When he returned to the truck, he drove back down the creek road toward the river and before long turned right under a huge sycamore into another lane. He forded the branch, went up by a stone chimney standing solitary on a little bench where a house had burned, and then down again to the disused barn of that place, and drove in. As before, he erased the few tire tracks that he had left in the lane. He stepped across the Katy's Branch Road and again disappeared into the woods.

While he did all this he had never ceased to whistle a barely audible whisper of a song, passing his breath in and out over the tip of his tongue.

The detective came walking out to the barn as if he were not sure where to put his feet. He was wearing shiny shoes with perforated toes, a tallish man, softening in the middle. He looked a little like somebody Lyda might have seen before. His dark hair was combed straight over his forehead in bangs. He walked with his left hand in his pocket, the jacket of his blue suit held back on that side.

Lyda herself was wearing a pair of rubber boots, but in expectation of company she had put on her best everyday dress. She was carrying two five-gallon buckets of corn that, as the detective approached, she emptied over the fence to the sows.

"Good morning. Mrs. Branch?" the detective said.

"Yes. Good morning."

The children were in the barn, doing the milking and the other chores, and Lyda, as she greeted the detective, started walking back toward the house.

He was showing her a badge. "Detective Kyle Bode of the state police, Mrs. Branch. I hope you'll be willing to answer a few questions."

Lyda laughed, looking out over the white cloud of fog that lay in the river valley. "I reckon I'll have to know what questions," she said.

"Well, you're Mrs. Danny Branch? And Danny Branch is Mr. Burley Coulter's next of kin?"

"That's right."

"And you're aware that Mr. Coulter has disappeared from his hospital room?"

"Yes."

"Is Mr. Branch at home?"

"No."

"Can you tell me where he went?"

"Well, he said something about Indiana."

"You don't know where?"

"Well, he sometimes goes up there to the Amish. You know, we farm with horses, and Danny has to depend on the Amish for harness and other things."

"Hmmm. Horses. Well," the detective said. "When did Mr. Branch leave?"

"I couldn't say."

"You don't know, or you don't remember?"

"I can't say that I do."

Lyda had not ceased to walk, nor he to walk with her, and now, as they were approaching the yard gate, the detective stopped. "Mrs. Branch, I have the distinct feeling that you are playing a little game with me. I think your husband has Mr. Coulter with him in Indiana—or wherever he is—and I think you know he does, and you're protecting him. Your husband, I would like to remind you, may be in very serious trouble with the law, and unless you cooperate you may be, too."

Lyda looked straight at him. Her eyes were an intense, surprising blue, and sometimes when she looked suddenly at you they seemed to leave little flashes of blue light dancing in the air. And the detective saw her then: a big woman, good-looking for her age, which was maybe forty or forty-five, and possessed of great practical strength (he remembered her tossing the contents of those heavy buckets over the fence), but her eyes, now that he looked at her, were what impressed him most. They were eyes not at all in the habit of concealment, but they certainly were in the habit of withstanding. They withstood him. They made him feel like explaining that he was only doing his duty.

"Mister," she said without any trace of fear that he could detect, "it scares me to be talking to the police. I never talked to the police before in my life. If you want to know any more, you'll have to talk to Henry Catlett down at Hargrave."

"Is Henry Catlett your lawyer?"

"Henry's our friend," she said.

"Yes," the detective said. "I'll go see him. Thank you very much for your time."

When Detective Bode walked away from Lyda, he already felt the mire of failure pulling at his feet. He had felt it before. Long ago, it seemed, he had studied to be a policeman because he wanted to become the kind of man who solved things. He had imagined himself becoming a man who—insightful, alert, and knowing—stepped into the midst of confusion and made clarity and order that people would be grateful for. So far, it had not turned out that way. He was twenty-nine years old already, and he had been confused as much as most people. In spite of the law and the government and the police, it seemed, people went right on and did whatever they were going to do. They had motives that were confusing, and they left evidence that was confusing. Sometimes they left no evidence. The science of crime solving was a clumsy business. Many criminals and many noncriminals were smarter than Kyle Bode—or, anyhow, smarter than Kyle Bode had been able to prove himself to be so far. He had begun to believe that he might end up as some kind of paper shuffler, had even begun to think that it might be a relief.

He had understood all too well, anyhow, the rather cynical grin with which his friend, Rich Ferris, had handed him this case. "Here's one that'll make you famous."

And what a case it was! Here was an old guy resting easy in the best medical facility money could buy. And what happened? This damned redneck, Danny Branch, who was his nephew or something, came and kidnapped him out of his hospital bed in the middle of the night. And took him off where? To Indiana? Not likely, Detective Bode thought. He would bet that Mr. Burley Coulter, alive or dead, and his kidnapper, Mr. Danny Branch, were somewhere just out of sight in some of these godforsaken hills and hollows.

Kyle Bode objected to hills and hollows. He objected to them especially if they were all overgrown with trees. They offended his sense of the way things ought to be. That the government of the streets and highways persisted in having business in hills and hollows and woods and briar patches in every kind of weather was no small part of his disillusionment.

And that big woman with her boots and her so-unimpressed blue eyes—it pleased him to believe that she was looking him straight in the eye and lying. In fact, he had wished a little that she would admire him, and he knew that she had not.

Traveling at a contemplative speed down the river road toward Hargrave, he glanced up at his image in the rearview mirror and patted down his hair.

Kyle Bode's father had originated in the broad bottomlands of a community called Nowhere, three counties west of Louisville. Under pressure from birth to "get out of here and make something out of yourself," Kyle's father had come to Louisville and worked his way into a farm equipment dealership. Kyle was the dealer's third child and second son. He might have succeeded to the dealership—"You boys can be partners," their father had said—but the older brother possessed an invincible practicality and a head start, and besides Kyle did not want to spend his life dealing with farmers. He had higher aims that made him dangerous to those he considered to be below him. Unlike his brother, Kyle was an idealist, with a little bit of an ambition to be a hero. Perhaps by the same token, he was also a man given to lethargy and to sudden onsets of violence by which he attempted to drive back whatever circumstances his lethargy had allowed to close in on him. Sagged and silent in his chair at a party or beer joint, he would suddenly thrust himself, with fists flying, at some spontaneously elected opponent. This did not happen often enough to damage him much, and it remained surprising to his friends.

Soon after graduation, he married his high school sweetheart. And then while he was beginning his career as a policeman, they, and especially he, began to dabble in some of the recreational sidelines of the countercultural revolution. He became sexually liberated. He suspected that his wife had experienced this liberation as well, but he did not catch her, and perhaps this was an ill omen for his police career. On the contrary, as it happened, she caught him in the very inflorescence of ecstasy on the floor of the carport of a house where they were attending a party. He was afraid for a while that she would divorce him, but when it became clear to him that she would not, he began to feel that she was limiting his development, and he divorced her in order to be free to be himself.

He cut quite a figure at parties after that. One festive night a young lady said, "Kyle, do you know who you really look like?" And he said, "No." And she said, "Ringo Starr." That was when he began to comb down his bangs. Girls and young women were always saying to him after that, "Do you know who you look like?" And he would say, "No. Who?" as if he had no notion what they were talking about.

His second wife, whom he married because he had made her pregnant—for he really was a conscientious young man who wanted to do the right thing—was proud of that resemblance, at first seriously and then jokingly, for a while. And then he ceased to remind her of anyone but himself, whereupon she divorced him.

He knew that she had not left him because she was dissatisfied with him but because she was not able to be satisfied for very long with anything. He disliked and feared this in her at the same time that he recognized it in himself. He, too, was dissatisfied; he could not see what he had because he was always looking around for something else. And so perhaps it was out of mutual dissatisfaction that their divorce had come, and now they were free. Perhaps even their little daughter was free, who was tied down no more than her parents were, for they sent her flying back and forth between them like a shuttlecock, and spoiled her in vying for her allegiance, and gave her more freedom of choice than she could have used well at twice her age. They were all free, he supposed. But finally he had had to ask if they were, any of them, better off than they had been and if they could hope to be better off than they were. For they were not satisfied. And by now he had to suppose, and to fear, that they were not going to be satisfied. He had become almost resigned to revolving for the rest of his life, somewhere beyond gravity, in the modern vortex of infatuation and divorce.

Surely there must be someplace to stop. In lieu of a more final place, though it was too early in the day to be thinking about it, he would take the lounge of the Outside Inn, the comers and goers shadowy between him and the neon, a filled and frosted glass in front of him, a slow brokenhearted song on the jukebox.

And maybe the mood would hit him to ask one of the women to dance. Angela, maybe, who admitted to being lonesome and liked to dance close. They would dance, they would move as one, and after a while he would let his right hand slide down, as if by accident, onto her hip. And he would say, "Oh, Angela, you make me feel like I might realize my full potential as an individual."

But his car, as though mindful of his duty when he was not, had taken him into Hargrave. He stopped for the first light and then turned to drive around the courthouse square; he was looking for a place to eat breakfast. The futility of this day insinuated itself into his thoughts, as unignorable as if it crawled palpably on his skin. Here he was, looking for a comatose old geezer who had (if Detective Bode mistook not) been abducted by his next of kin, who, if the old geezer died, would be guilty of a crime that probably had not even been named yet. Maybe he was about to turn up something totally new in the annals of crime, though he would just as soon turn it up someplace else. In fact, he would just as soon somebody else turned it up. It ought, he told himself, to be easy enough to turn up, for it was clearly the work of an amateur. And yet this amateur, who had had the gall or stupidity or foolishness or whatever it took to kidnap his victim right out of the middle of a busy hospital, had managed to be seen, and not clearly seen at that, by only one witness and had left no evidence. So Detective Bode was working from a coincidence, a good guess, and no evidence. His success, he supposed, depended on the improbable occurrence of a lucky moment in which he would be able to outsmart the self-styled "country lawyer of sorts," Henry Catlett.

"Later for that," Kyle Bode thought.

Among the dilapidating storefronts he found the place he thought he remembered, the Front Street Grill, and he parked and went in.

When Lyda had called, Nathan and Hannah were just waking up. Before Nathan turned the light on by the bed, they could see the gray early daylight out the window. After Nathan went to the phone, Hannah lay still and listened, but from Nathan's brief responses she could not make out who had called.

She heard Nathan hang up the phone. He came back into the bedroom and told her carefully everything that Lyda had told him.

"But wait," she said. "What's happening? Where *is* Danny?"

"We'd better not help each other answer those questions, Hannah—not for a while, anyhow."

He opened a drawer of the bureau and took out one of his shirts, a green one.

"Where are *you* going?"

He smiled at her. "I'll be back before long."

Though Nathan was a quiet man, he was not usually a secretive one. But she asked no more.

He went out. She heard him go through the kitchen and out the back door. She heard the pickup start and go out the driveway. And then the sound of it was gone.

Usually, after Nathan got up, there would be a few minutes when she could stay in bed, sometimes rolling over into the warmth where he had slept, before she got up to start breakfast. She loved that time. She would lie still, listening, as the night ended and the day began. She heard the first bird songs of the morning. She heard Nathan leave the house, the milk bucket ringing a little as he took it down from its nail on the back porch. She heard the barn door slide open, and then Nathan's voice calling the cows, and then the cowbells coming up through the pale light. If she got up when the cows reached the barn, she could have breakfast ready by the time Nathan came back to the house.

But this morning, as soon as the truck was out of earshot, she got up. For there was much to think about, much to do and to be prepared for. Now that she was fully awake, she had, like the others, caught the drift of what was happening.

She took the milk bucket and went to the barn and milked and did the chores, the things that Nathan usually did, and then she went to open the henhouse and put out feed and water for the hens—her work. At the house, she strained the milk, set the table for breakfast and got out the food. But Nathan was not back. She sat down by the kitchen window where she could see him when he came in. She kept her sewing basket there and the clothes that needed mending. But now, though she took a piece of sewing onto her lap, she did not work. She sat with her hands at rest, looking out the window as the mists of the hollows turned whiter under the growing light. She wanted to be thinking of Burley, but amongst all the knowing and unknowing of this strangely begun day she could not think of him. Who was most on her mind now was Nathan, and she wished him home.

It was home to her, this house, though once it had not been, nor had this neighborhood been. She had come to Port William thirty-five years ago. She had married Virgil Feltner as war spread across the world, and had lived with him for a little while in the household of his parents, before he was called into the service. When he left, because her own parents were dead and Mat and Margaret Feltner had made her welcome, she stayed on with them, and they were mother and father to her. In the summer of 1944, Virgil came home on leave; he and Hannah were together a little while again, and when he went back to his unit she was with child.

The life that Hannah had begun to live came to an end when her young husband was killed, and for a while it seemed that she had no life except in the child that she had borne into the world of one death and of many. And then Nathan had called her out of that world into the living world again, and a new life had come to her; she and Nathan had made and shaped it, welcomed its additions and borne its losses, together. They moved to this place that Nathan had bought when he returned from the war. Run-down and thicket-grown as it was, its possibility had beckoned to him and then to her. They had moved into the old house, restored it while they lived in it and while they restored the farm; they had raised their children here. And they were son and daughter both to Margaret and Mat Feltner and to Nathan's father, whose oldest son, Tom, had also been killed in the war.

They had raised their children, sent them to college, seen them go away to work in cities, and, though wishing they might have stayed, wished them well. Their children had gone, and over the years, one by one, so had their elders. And each one of these departures had left them with more work to do and, as Hannah sometimes thought, less reason to do it.

They were in their fifties now, farming three farms simply because there was no one else to do it. In addition to the Feltner Place and their own, they were also farming Nathan's home place, which he had inherited from his father. Like everybody else still farming, they were spread too thin, and help was hard to find. The Port William neighborhood had as many people, probably, as it had ever had, but it did not have them where it needed them. It had a good many of them now on little city lots carved out of farms, from which they commuted to city jobs. Nathan and Hannah were overburdened, too tired at the end of every day, and with no relief in sight. And yet they did not think of quitting. Nathan worked through his long days steadily and quietly. Some days Hannah worked with him; when she needed help, he helped her. They had two jersey cows for milk and butter; they raised and slaughtered their meat hogs; they kept a flock of hens; they raised a garden. And still, in spite of all, there were quietnesses that they came to, in which they rested and were together and were glad to be.

And though their loneliness had increased, they were not alone. Of the membership of kin and friends that had held them always, some had died and some had gone, but some remained. There were Lyda and Danny Branch and their children. There were Arthur and Martin Rowanberry. After Elton Penn's death, his son Jack had continued to farm their place, and Mary Penn was living in Hargrave, still a friend. There were the various Catletts, who, whatever else they were, were still farmers and still of the membership: Bess and Wheeler who were now old, Sarah and Henry and their children, Flora and Andy and theirs.

When she thought of their neighborhood, Hannah wondered whether or not to count the children. Like the old, the young were leaving. The old were dying without successors, and Hannah was aware how anxiously those who remained had begun to look into the eyes of the children. They were watching not just their own children now but anybody's children. For as the burden of keeping the land increased for the always fewer who remained, as the difference continued to increase between the price of what they had to sell and the cost of what they had to buy, they knew that they had less and less to offer the children, and fewer arguments to make.

They held on, she and those others, who might be the last. They held on, and they held out, and they were seeing, perhaps, a little more clearly what they had to hold out against. Every year, it seemed to her, they were living more from what they could do for themselves and each other and less from what they had to buy. Nathan's refusals to buy things, she had noticed, were becoming firmer as well as more frequent. "No," he would say, "I guess we can get along without that." "No. Not at that price." "No. I reckon the old one will run a while longer." And though he spoke these answers kindly enough, there was no doubting their finality. Nobody ever asked twice.

Maybe, she thought, this was Danny's influence. Danny was eight years younger than Nathan, and it was strange to think that Nathan could have been influenced by him, but maybe he had been. Danny never had belonged much to the modern world, and every year he appeared to belong to it less. Of them all, Danny most clearly saw that world as his enemy—as *their* enemy—and most forthrightly and cheerfully repudiated it. He reserved his allegiance to his friends and his place.

Danny was the right one for the rescue that Hannah did not doubt was being accomplished, though she did not know quite how. He had some grace about him that would permit him to accomplish it with joy. She smiled, for she knew, too, that Danny was a true son to Burley, not only in loyalty but in nature—that he had shared fully in that half of Burley's life that had belonged to the woods and the darkness. Nathan, she thought, had understood that side of Burley and been friendly to it without so much taking part in it. Nathan would hunt or fish with

Burley and Danny occasionally and would enjoy it, but he was more completely a farmer than they were, more content to be bound within the cycle of the farmer's year. You never felt, looking at him, that he had left something somewhere beyond the cleared fields that he would be bound to go back and get. He did not have that air that so often hung about Danny and Burley, suggesting that they might suddenly look back, grin and wave, and disappear among the trees. He was as solid, as frankly and fully present as the doorstep, a man given to work and to quiet—like, she thought, his father.

They were her study, those Coulter men. Figuring them out was her need, her way of loving them, and sometimes her amusement. The one who most troubled her had been Nathan's father, Jarrat—a driven, workbrittle, weather-hardened, lonely, and nearly wordless man, who went to his grave without completing his sorrow for his young wife who had died when their sons were small, whom he never mentioned and never forgot. His death had left in Hannah an unused and yearning tenderness.

Burley lived in a larger world than his brother had lived in, and not just because, as a hunter and a woods walker, he readily crossed boundaries that had confined Jarrat. Burley was a man freely in love with freedom and with pleasures, who watched the world with an amused, alert eye to see what it would do next, and if the world did not seem inclined to get on very soon to anything of interest, he gave it his help. Hannah's world had been made dearer to her by Burley's laughter, his sometimes love of talk (his own and other people's), and his delight in outrageous behavior (his own as a young man and other people's). She knew that Burley had his sorrows. She knew he grieved that he had not married Kate Helen Branch, Danny's mother, and that he regretted his late acknowledgment of Danny as his son. But she knew, too, how little he had halted in grief and regret, how readily and cheerfully he had gone on, however burdened, to whatever had come next. And because he was never completely of her world, she had the measure of his generosity to her and the others. Though gifted for disappearance, he had never entirely disappeared but had been with them to the end.

And now the thought of him did return to her. As he had grown sicker and weaker, the thought of him had come more and more into her keeping, and she had received it with her love and her thanks as she had received her children when they were newborn.

She thought it strange and wonderful that she had been given all these to love. She thought it a blessing that she had loved them to the limit of her grief at parting with them, and that grief had only deepened and clarified her love. Since her first grief had brought her fully to birth and wakefulness in this world, an unstinting compassion had moved in her, like a live stream flowing deep underground, by which she knew herself and others and the world. It was her truest self, that stream always astir inside her that was at once pity and love, knowledge and faith, forgiveness, grief, and joy. It made her fearful, and it made her unafraid.

Like the others, she had mourned her uselessness to Burley in his sickness. Like the others, she had been persuaded and had helped to persuade that they should get help for him. Like the others, once they had given him into the power of the doctors and into the sterile, hard light of that way and place in which he did not belong, she had wanted him back. And she had held him to her in her thoughts, loving the old, failed flesh and bone of him as never before, as if she could feel, in thought, in nerve, and through all intervening time and distance, the little helpless child that he had been and had become again. Knowing now that he was with Danny, hidden away, somewhere at home, joy shook her and the window blurred in her sight.

She heard, after a while, the tires of Nathan's truck on the gravel, and then the truck came into sight, stopped in its usual place, and Nathan got out. She watched him as he walked to the house, not so light-stepping as he used to be. She knew that as he walked, looking alertly around, he would be whistling over and over a barely audible little thread of a tune.

When he came in and she looked at him from the stove, where she had gone to start their breakfast, he smiled at her. "Don't ask," he said.

She said, "I will only ask one question. Are you worried about Uncle Burley?"

"No," he said, and he smiled at her again.

Henry hurried up the steps to the office, knowing that his father would already be there. Wheeler came to the office early, an hour maybe before Henry and the secretary, because, as Henry supposed, he liked to be there by himself. It was a place of haste and sometimes of turmoil, that office, where they worked at one problem knowing that another was waiting and sometimes that several others were waiting. Wheeler would come there in the quiet of the early morning to meet the day on his own terms. He would sit down at his desk covered with opened books, thick folders of papers and letters, ruled yellow pads covered with his impulsive blue script, and with one of those pads on his lap and a pen in his hand he would call the coming day to order in his mind.

He had been at work there for more than fifty years. In all that time the look of the place had changed more by accretion than by alteration. There were three rooms: Wheeler's office in the front, overlooking the courthouse square; Henry's in the back, overlooking an alley and some backyards; and, between the two, a waiting room full of bookcases and chairs where the secretary, Hilda Roe, had her desk.

Wheeler was sitting at his desk with his hat on, his back to the door. He was leaning back in his chair, his right ankle crossed over his left knee, and he was writing in fitful jabs on a yellow pad. Henry tapped on the facing of the door.

"Come in," Wheeler said without looking up.

Henry came in.

"Sit down," Wheeler said.

Henry did not sit down.

"What you got on your mind?" Wheeler asked.

"Burley Coulter disappeared from the hospital last night."

Wheeler swiveled his chair around and gave Henry a

look that it had taken Henry thirty years to meet with composure. "Where's Danny Branch?"

Henry grinned. "Danny's away from home. Lyda said he said something about Indiana."

"You've talked to the police?"

"Yes. And a state police detective, Mr. Kyle Bode, has already been to see Lyda."

Wheeler wrote Kyle Bode's name on the yellow pad. "What did you find out?"

"Somebody went into Burley's room at some time around two o'clock. Whoever it was disconnected him from the life machines, loaded him onto a gurney, and escaped with him 'into the night,' as they say. They found no fingerprints or other evidence. They have found one witness, a nurse, who saw 'a huge man' wearing a blue shirt going up on an elevator with an empty gurney and then down with what she thought was a dead person."

"We don't know anybody huge, do we?" Wheeler said. "What about the blue shirt?"

"Don't know," Henry said.

"Do you know this Detective Bode?"

"I had a little talk with him once, over in the court room."

"You're expecting him?"

"Yes."

Wheeler spread his hands palms down on his lap, studied them a moment, and then looked up again. "Well, what are you going to do?"

"Don't know," Henry said. "I guess I'll have to wait to find out. I've told Lyda and everybody else concerned to come here as soon as they can. And I think you ought to call Mother and Mary Penn and tell them to come. I don't want the police to talk to any more of them alone."

This time it was Wheeler who grinned. He reached for the phone. "All right, my boy."

Working with the spade, Danny cut into the ground the long and narrow outline of the grave. It was hard digging, the gentle rain of the night not having penetrated very far, and there were tree roots and rocks. Danny soon settled into a rhythm in keeping with the length and difficulty of the job. He used the spud bar to loosen the dirt, cut the roots, and pry out the rocks. With the spade he piled the loosened dirt on one side of the grave; with his hands he laid the rocks out on the other side. He worked steadily, stopping only to return to the barn to verify that the sleeper there did not wake. On each visit he stood by Burley only long enough to touch him and to say, "You're all right. You don't have to worry about a thing." Each time, he saw that Burley's breath came more shallow and more slow.

And finally, on one of these trips to the barn, he knew as he entered the doorway that the breaths had stopped, and he stopped, and then went soundlessly in where the body lay. It looked unaccountably small. Now of its long life in this place there remained only this small artifact of flesh and bone. In the hospital, Burley's body had seemed to Danny to be off in another world; he had not been able to rid himself of the feeling that he was looking at it through a lens or a window. Here, the old body seemed to belong to this world absolutely, it was so accepting now of all that had come to it, even its death. Burley had died as he had slept—he had not moved. Danny leaned and picked up the still hands and laid them together.

He went back to his digging and worked on as before. As he accepted again the burden of the work and measured his thoughts to it, Burley returned to his mind, and he knew him again as he had been when his life was full. He saw again the stance and demeanor of the man, the amused eyes, the lips pressed together while speech waited upon thought, an almost inviolable patience in the set of the shoulders. It was as though Burley stood in full view nearby, at ease and well at home—as though Danny could see him, but only on the condition that he not look.

When Detective Bode climbed the stairs to the office of Catlett & Catlett, the waiting room was deserted. Through the open door at the rear of the room, he could see Henry with his feet propped on his desk, reading the morning paper. Kyle Bode closed the waiting room door somewhat loudly.

Henry looked up. "Come in," he called. He got up to meet his visitor, who shook his hand and then produced a badge.

"Kyle Bode, state police."

Henry gave him a warm and friendly smile. "Sure," he said. "I remember you. Have a seat. What can I do for you?"

The detective sat down in the chair that Henry positioned for him. He had not smiled. He waited for Henry, too, to sit down. "I'm here in connection with what I suppose would be called a kidnapping. A man named Burley Coulter, of Port William, was removed from his hospital room without authorization at about two o'clock this morning."

"So I heard!" Henry said. "Lyda Branch called me about it. I figured you fellows would have made history of this case by now. You mean you haven't?"

"Not yet," Kyle Bode said. "It's not all that clear-cut, probably due to the unprecedented nature of the crime."

"You show me an unprecedented crime," Henry said, falling in with the detective's philosophical tone. "Kidnapping, you said?"

"It's a crime involving the new medical technology. I mean, some of this stuff is unheard of. We're living in the future right now. I figure this crime is partly motivated by anxiety about this new stuff. Like maybe the guy that did it is some kind of religious nut."

Henry put his dark-rimmed reading glasses back on and made his face long and solemn, tilting his head back, as he was apt to do when amused in exalted circumstances. "In the past, too," he said.

"What?"

"If we're living in the future, then surely we're living in the past, too, and the dead and the unborn are right here in our midst. Wouldn't you say so?"

"I guess so," Kyle Bode said.

"Well," Henry said, "do you have any clues as to the possible identity of the perpetrator of this crime?"

"Yes, as a matter of fact, we do. We have a good set of fingerprints."

Kyle Bode spoke casually, looking at the fingernails of his right hand, which he held in his left. When he looked up to gauge the effect, not the Henry of their recent philosophical exchange but an altogether different Henry, one he had encountered before, was looking at him point-blank, the glasses off.

"Mr. Bode," Henry said, "that was a lie you just told. As a matter of fact, you don't have any evidence. If we are going to get along, you had better assume that I know as much about this case as you do. Now, what do you want?"

Kyle Bode felt a sort of chill crawl up the back of his neck and over the top of his head, settling for an exquisite moment among his hair roots. He maintained his poise, however, and was pleased to note that he was returning Henry's look. And the right question came to him.

"I want to find the victim's nephew, Danny Branch. Do you know where he is?"

"Son," Henry said. "The victim's son. I only know what his wife told me."

"What did she tell you?"

"She said he said something about Indiana."

"We have an APB on him in Indiana." Detective Bode said this with the air of one who leaves no stone unturned. "But we really think—*I* think—the solution is to be found right here."

But looking at Henry and remembering Lyda, he felt unmistakably the intimation that he and his purpose were not trusted. These people did not trust him, and they were not going to trust him. He felt his purpose unraveling in his failure to have their trust. In default of that trust, *every* stone must be turned. And it was a rocky country. He knew he had already failed—unless, by some fluke of luck, he could find somebody to outsmart. Or, maybe, unless this Danny Branch should appear wearing a blue shirt.

"Maybe you can tell me," he said, "if Danny Branch is Mr. Coulter's heir."

"Burley was—is—my father's client," Henry said. "You ought to ask him about that. Danny, I reckon, is my client."

The detective made his tone more reasonable, presuming somewhat upon his and Henry's brotherhood in the law: "Mr. Catlett, I'd like to be assured of your cooperation in this case. After all, it will be in your client's best interest to keep this from going as far as it may go."

"Can't help you," Henry said.

"You mean that you, a lawyer, won't cooperate with the law of the state in the solution of a crime?"

"Well, you see, it's a matter of patriotism."

"Patriotism? You can't mean that."

"I mean patriotism—love for your country and your neighbors. There's a difference, Mr. Bode, between the state, or any other organization, and the country. I'm not going to cooperate with you in this case because I don't like what you represent in this case."

"What I represent? What do you think I represent?"

"The organization of the world."

"And what does that mean?" In spite of himself, and

not very coolly, Detective Bode was lapsing into the tone of mere argument, perhaps of mere self-defense.

"It means," Henry said, "that you want whatever you know to serve power. You want knowledge to *be* power. And you'll make your ignorance count, too, if you can be deceitful and clever enough. You think everything has to be explained to your superiors and concealed from your inferiors. For instance, you just lied to me with a clear conscience, as a way of serving justice. What I stand for can't survive in the world you're helping to make, Mr. Bode." Henry was grinning, enjoying himself, and now he allowed the detective to see that he was.

"Are you some kind of anarchist?" the detective said. "Just what the hell are you, anyway?"

"I'm a patriot, like I said. I'm a man who's not going to cooperate with you on this case. You're here to represent the right of the state and other large organizations to decide for us and come between us. The people you represent will come out here, without asking our opinion, and shut down a barbershop or a little slaughterhouse because it's not sanitary enough for us, and then let other businesses—richer ones—poison the air and water."

"What's *that* got to do with it?"

"Listen," Henry said. "I'm trying to explain something to you. I'm not the only one who won't cooperate with you in your search for Danny Branch. There are several of us here who aren't reconciled to the loss of any good thing. We know that for a hundred years, the chief clients and patrons of that state of yours have been in the business of robbing and impoverishing the country people and their places."

"I'm not in charge of the state," Kyle Bode said. "I'm just doing my duty."

"And you're here now to tell us that a person who is sick and unconscious, or even a person who is conscious and well, is ultimately a property of the organizations and the state. Aren't you?" Henry was still grinning.

"It wasn't authorized. He asked nobody's permission. He told nobody. He signed no papers. It was a crime. You can't let people just walk around and do what they want to like that. He didn't even pay the bill."

"Some of us think people belong to each other and to God," Henry said. "Are you going to let a hospital keep a patient hostage until he pays his bill? You were *against* kidnapping a while ago."

Detective Bode was resting his brow in the palm of his hand. He was shaking his head. When it became clear that Henry was finished, the detective looked up. "Mr. Catlett, if I may, I would like to talk to your father."

"Sure," Henry said, getting up. "You going to tell on me?"

And only then, finally, did Detective Bode smile.

Danny dug the grave down until he stood hip deep in it. And then he dug again until it was past waist deep. And then, putting his hands on the ground beside it, he leapt out of it, and stood looking down into it, and thought. The grave was somewhat longer than Burley had been tall; it was widened at the middle to permit Danny to stand in it to lay the body down; it was deep enough.

Using the larger flagstones that he had taken from the grave and bringing more from the creek, Danny shaped a long, narrow box in the bottom of the grave. Digging to varying depths to seat the stones upright with their straightest edges aligned at the top, he worked his way from the head of the grave to the foot and back again, tamping each stone tightly into place. The light beams that came through the heavy foliage shifted slowly from one opening to another, and slowly they became more perpendicular. The day grew warmer, and Danny paused now and again to wipe the sweat from his face. Again he went to the spring and drank, and returned to his work. The crickets sang steadily, and the creek made its constant little song over the rocks. Within those sounds and the larger quiet that included them, now and then a woodpecker drummed or called or a jay screamed or a squirrel barked. In the stillness a few leaves let go and floated down. And always Danny could smell the fresh, moist earth of the grave.

When he had finished placing the upright stones, he paved the floor of the grave, laying the broad slabs level and filling the openings that remained with smaller stones. He made good work of it, though it would be seen in all the time of the world only by him and only for a little while. He put the shape of the stone casket together as if the stones had made a casket once before and had been scattered, and now he had found them and pieced them together again.

He carried up more stones from the creek, the biggest he could handle. These would be the capstones, and he laid them in stacks at the head and foot of the grave. It was ready now. He went down to the barn and removed the blankets that covered Burley and withdrew the pillow from under his head. He folded the blankets into a pallet on the paved floor of the grave and placed the pillow at its head.

When he carried Burley to the grave, he went up by the gentlest, most open way so that there need be no haste or struggle or roughness, for now they had come to the last of the last things. A heavy pressure of finality swelled in his heart and throat as if he might have wept aloud, but as he walked he made no sound. He stepped into the grave and laid the body down. He composed it like a sleeper, laying the hands together as before. And the body seemed to accept again its stillness and its deep sleep, submissive to the motion of the world until the world's end. Danny brought up the rest of the bedclothes and laid them over Burley, covering, at last, his face.

As before, the thought returned to him that he was not acting only for himself. He thought of Lyda and Hannah and Nathan and the others, and he went down along the creek and then up across the thickety north slope on the other side, gathering flowers as he went. He picked spires of goldenrod, sprays of farewell-summer and of lavender, gold-centered asters; he picked yellow late sunflowers, the white-starred flower heads of snakeroot with their odor of warm honey, and finally, near the creek, the triple-lobed, deep blue flowers of great lobelia. Stepping into the grave again, he covered the shrouded body with these, their bright colors and their weedy scent warm from the sun, laying them down in shingle fashion so that the blossoms were always uppermost, until the grave seemed at last to contain a small garden in bloom. And then, having touched Burley for the last time, he laid across the upright sides of the coffin the broad covering stones, first one layer, and then another over the cracks in the first.

He lifted himself out of the grave and stood at the foot of it. He let the quiet reassemble itself around him, the quiet of the place now one with that of the old body sleeping in its grave. Into that great quiet he said aloud, "Be with him, as he has been with us." And then he began to fill the grave.

Henry rapped on his father's door and then pushed it open. Wheeler was still wearing his hat, but now he was holding the telephone receiver in his right hand. His right arm was extended at full length, propped on the arm of his chair. Both Henry and Kyle Bode could hear somebody insistently and plaintively explaining something through the phone. When the door opened, Wheeler looked around.

"Detective Bode would like to talk with you."

Wheeler acknowledged Henry with a wave of his left hand. To Kyle Bode he said, "Come in, sir," and gestured toward an empty chair.

Kyle Bode came in and sat down.

Wheeler put the receiver to his mouth and ear and said, "But I *know* what your problem is, Mr. Hernshaw. You've told me several times . . ." The voice never stopped talking. Wheeler shifted the receiver to his left hand, clamping his palm over the mouthpiece, and, smiling, offered his right hand to the detective. "I'm glad to know you, Mr. Bode. I'll get done here in a minute." He dangled the receiver out over his chair arm again while he and Kyle Bode listened to it, its tone of injury and wearied explanation as plain as if they could make out the words. And then they heard it say distinctly, "*So. Here is what I think.*"

In the portentous pause that followed, Wheeler quickly raised the receiver and said into it with an almost gentle patience, "But, Mr. Hernshaw, as I have explained to you a number of times, what you think is of no account, because you are not going to get anybody else on the face of the earth to think it."

Something was said then that Wheeler interrupted: "No. A verbal agreement is *not* a contract if there were no witnesses and you are the only one who can remember it. Now you think about it. I can't talk to you anymore this morning because I've got a young fellow waiting to see me."

He paused again, listening, and then said, "Yessir. Thank you. It's always good to talk with you." He hung up.

"That was Walter Hernshaw," he said to Kyle Bode. "Like many of my friends, he has got old. I've had that very conversation with him the last four Saturdays. And I'll tell you something: if I sent him a bill for my time —which, of course, I won't, because he hasn't hired me, and because I won't be hired by him—he would be amazed. Because he thinks that if he conducts his business on Saturday by telephone, it's not work. Now what can I do for you?"

The detective cleared his throat. "I assume you're aware, Mr. Catlett, that Mr. Burley Coulter was taken from his hospital room early this morning by some unauthorized person."

"Yes," Wheeler said. "Henry told me, and I'm greatly concerned about it. Burley is a cousin of mine, you know."

"No," the detective said, feeling another downward swerve of anxiety. "I didn't."

"Yes," Wheeler said, "his father and my father were first cousins. They were the grandchildren of Amos Abner Coulter, who was the son of Jonas T. Coulter, who was, I reckon, one of the first white people to come into this country. Well, have you people figured out how Burley was taken by this unauthorized person?"

"He just went in with a gurney," Kyle Bode said, "and loaded Mr. Coulter onto it, and covered him up to look like a corpse, and took him away—right through the middle of a busy hospital. Can you believe the audacity of it?"

"Sure, I believe it," Wheeler said. "But I've seen a lot of audacity in my time. It's not as hard for me to believe as it used to be. Do you know who did this? Do you have clear evidence?"

"As a matter of fact, we don't. But we have a good idea who did it."

"Who?"

"Danny Branch—who is, I'm told, Mr. Coulter's son?"

"That's right," Wheeler said. "And you're wondering why he doesn't have his father's name." Wheeler then told why Danny went by the name of Branch, his mother's name, rather than Coulter, which was a long and somewhat complicated story to which the detective quit listening.

"Anyhow," Kyle Bode said, "Danny Branch seems also to have disappeared. I wonder, Mr. Catlett, if you have any idea where he might have gone."

"I only know what Henry says Danny's wife told him."

"And what did she tell him?"

"He said she said he said something about Indiana."

"The Indiana police are watching for him," Kyle Bode said. "But a much likelier possibility is that he's somewhere around here—and that his father, alive or dead, is with him."

"You're assuming, I see, that Danny Branch is the guilty party." Wheeler smiled at the detective as he would perhaps have smiled at a grandson. "And what are you going to charge him with—impersonating an undertaker?"

Kyle Bode did not smile back. "Kidnapping, to start with. And, after that, if Mr. Coulter dies, maybe manslaughter."

"Well," Wheeler said. "That's serious."

"Mr. Catlett, is Danny Branch Mr. Coulter's heir?" The detective was now leaning forward somewhat aggressively in his seat.

Wheeler smiled again, seeing (and, Kyle Bode thought, appreciating) the direction of the detective's thinking. "Yes," he said. "He is."

"That makes it more likely, doesn't it?" Kyle Bode was getting the feeling that Wheeler was talking to him at such length because he liked his company. He corrected that by wondering if Wheeler, elderly as he was, knew that he was talking to a detective. He corrected that by glancing at the writing pad that Wheeler had tossed onto his desk. On one blue line of the pad he saw, inscribed without a quiver, "Det. Kyle Bode."

"Now your logic is pretty good there, Mr. Bode," Wheeler said. "You've got something there that you certainly will want to think about. A man sick and unconscious, dependent on life-prolonging machinery, surely is a pretty opportunity for the medical people. 'For wheresoever the carcase is, there will the eagles be gathered together.' You suspect Danny Branch of experiencing a coincidence of compassion and greed in this case. And of course that suspicion exactly mirrors the suspicion that attaches to the medical profession."

"But they were keeping him alive," Kyle Bode said. "Isn't that something?"

"It's something," Wheeler said. "It's not enough. There are many degrees and kinds of being alive. And some are worse than death."

"But they were doing their duty."

"Oh, yes," Wheeler said, "they were doing their solemn duty, as defined by themselves. And they were getting luxuriously paid. They were being merciful and they were getting rich. Let us not forget that one of the subjects of our conversation is money—the money to be spent and made in the art of medical mercy. Once the machinery gets into it, then the money gets into it. Once the money is there, then come the damned managers and the damned insurers and (I am embarrassed to say) the damned lawyers, not to mention the damned doctors who were there for the money before anybody. Before long the patient is hostage to his own cure. The beneficiary is the chattel of his benefactors.

"And first thing you know, you've got some poor sufferer all trussed up in a hospital, tied and tubed and doped and pierced with needles, who will never draw another breath for his own benefit and who may breathe on for years. It's a bad thing to get paid for, Mr. Bode, especially if you're in the business of mercy and healing and the relief of suffering.

"So there certainly is room for greed and mercy of another kind. I don't doubt that Danny, assuming he is the guilty party, has considered the cost; he's an intelligent man. Even so, I venture to say to you that you're wrong about him, insofar as you suspect him of acting out of greed. I'll give you two reasons that you had better consider. In the first place, he loves Burley. In the second place, he's not alone, and he knows it. You're thinking of a world in which legatee stands all alone, facing legator who has now become a mere obstruction between legatee and legacy. But you have thought up the wrong world. There are several of us here who belong to Danny and to whom he belongs, and we'll stand by him, whatever happens. Whatever happens, he and his family will have a place, and he knows it. After money, you know, we are talking about the question of the ownership of people. To whom and to what does Burley Coulter belong? If, as you allege, Danny Branch has taken Burley Coulter out of the hospital, he has done it because Burley belongs to him."

Wheeler was no longer making any attempt to speak to the point of Kyle Bode's visit, or if he was Kyle Bode no longer saw the point. And he had begun to hear, while Wheeler talked, the sounds of the gathering of several people in the adjoining room: the opening and shutting of the outer door, the scraping of feet and of chair legs, the murmur of conscientiously subdued voices.

Kyle Bode waved his hand at Wheeler and interrupted. "But he can't just carry him off without the hospital staff's permission."

"Why not?" Wheeler said. "A fellow would need their permission, I reckon, to get in. If he needs their permission to get out, he's in jail. Would you grant a proprietary right, or even a guardianship, to a hospital that you would not grant to a man's own son? I would oppose that, whatever the law said."

"Well, anyway," Detective Bode said, "all I know is that the law has been broken, and I am here to serve the law."

"But, my dear boy, you don't eat or drink the law, or sit in the shade of it or warm yourself by it, or wear it, or have your being in it. The law exists only to serve."

"Serve what?"

"Why, all the many things that are above it. Love."

Danny stood in the grave as he filled it, tamping the dirt in. The day in its sounding brightness stood around him. He kept to the rhythm he had established at the beginning, stopping only one more time to go to the spring for a drink. Though he sweated at his work, the day was comfortable, the suggestion of autumn palpably in the air, and he made good time.

As he filled the grave and thus slowly rose out of it, he felt again that the living man, Burley Coulter, was near him, watching and visible, except where he looked. The intimation of Burley's presence was constantly with him, at once troubling and consoling; in its newness, it kept him close to tears. It was as though he were being watched by a shy bird that remained, with uncanny fore-knowledge, just beyond the edge of vision, whichever way he looked.

When the grave was filled, he spread and leveled the surplus dirt. He gathered leaves and scattered them over the dirt and brushed over them lightly with a leafy branch. From twenty feet, only a practiced and expectant eye would have noticed the disturbance. After the dewfall or frost of one night, it would be harder to see. After the leaves fell, there would be no trace.

He carried his tools down to the barn, folded the pot and skillet and the piece of jowl and the cornmeal into his hunting coat, making a bundle that he could sling over his shoulder as before. Again using a leafy branch, he brushed out his tracks in the dust of the barn floor. He sprinkled dust and then water over the ashes of his fire. When his departure was fully prepared, he brought water from the spring and sat down and ate quickly the rest of the food he had prepared at breakfast.

By the time he left, the place had again resumed its quiet, and he walked away without disturbing it.

The absence of his truck startled Danny when he got

back to where he had left it, but he stood still only for a moment before he imagined what had happened. If the wrong people had found the truck, they would have come on up the branch and found him and Burley. The right person could only have been Nathan, who would have known where the key was hidden and who would have taken the truck to the nearest unlikely place where he could put it out of sight. And so Danny shouldered his tools and his bundle again and went to the road.

The road was not much traveled. Only one car passed, and Danny avoided it by stepping in among the tall horseweeds that grew between the roadside and the creek. When he came to the lane that branched off under the big sycamore, he turned without hesitation into it, knowing he was right when he got to the first muddy patch where Nathan had scuffed out the tire tracks. And yet he smiled when he stepped through the door of the old barn and saw his truck. He laid his tools in with the other fencing tools in the back, and then, opening the passenger door to toss in his bundle, he saw Nathan's green shirt lying on the seat. He smiled again and took off the blue shirt he was wearing and put the green one on. He thought of burning the blue shirt, but he did not want to burn it. It was a good shirt. A derelict washing machine was leaning against the wall of the barn just inside the upper doorway, and he tossed the shirt into it. He would come back for it in a few days.

When he got home and went into the kitchen, he found Lyda's note on the table.

"We are all at Henry's and Wheeler's office," she had

written. "Henry says for you to come, too, if you get back." And then she had crossed out the last phrase and added, "I reckon you are back."

Wheeler talked at ease, leaning back in his chair, his fingers laced over his vest, telling stories of the influence of the medical industry upon the local economy. He spoke with care, forming his sentences as if he were writing them down and looking at Kyle Bode all the time, with the apparent intent to instruct him.

"And so it has become possible," Wheeler said, "for one of our people to spend a long life accumulating a few thousand dollars by the hardest kind of work, only to have it entirely taken away by two or three hours in an operating room and a week or two in a hospital."

Listening, the detective became more and more anxious to regain control at least of his own participation in whatever it was that was going on. But he was finding the conversation difficult to interrupt not only because of the peculiar force that Wheeler's look and words put into it but because he did not much want to interrupt it. There was a kind of charm in the old man's earnest wish that the young man should be instructed. And when the young man did from time to time break into the conversation, it was to ask a question relative only to the old man's talk—questions that the young man, to his consternation, actually wanted to know the old man's answer to.

Finally the conversation was interrupted by Wheeler himself. "I believe we have some people here whom you'll want to see. They are Burley's close kin and close friends, the people who know him best. Come and meet them."

Kyle Bode had not been able to see where he was going for some time, and now suddenly he did see, and he saw that *they* had seen where he was going all along and had got there ahead of him. His mind digressed into relief that he was assigned to this case alone, that none of his colleagues could see his confusion. Conscientiously—though surely not conscientiously enough—he had sought the order that the facts of the case would make. And not only had he failed so far to achieve that clear and explainable order but he had been tempted over and over again into the weakness of self-justification. Worse than that, he had been tempted over and over again to leave, with Wheeler, the small, clear world of the law and its explanations and to enter the larger, darker world not ordered by human reasons or subject to them, in which he sensed obscurely that something might live that he, too, might be glad to have alive.

Standing with his right arm outstretched and then with his hand spread hospitably on Kyle Bode's back, Wheeler gathered him toward the door, which he opened onto a room now full of people, all of whom fell silent and looked expectantly at the detective as though he might have been a long-awaited guest of honor.

Guided still by Wheeler's hand on his back, Kyle Bode turned toward the desk to the left of the stairway door, at which sat a smiling young woman who held a stenographer's pad and pencil on her lap.

"This is Detective Kyle Bode, ladies and gentlemen,"

Wheeler said. "Mr. Bode, this is Hilda Roe, our secretary."

Hilda extended her hand to Kyle Bode, who shook it cordially.

Wheeler pressed him on to the left. "This is Sarah Catlett, Henry's wife.

"This is my wife, Bess.

"This is Mary Penn.

"This is Art Rowanberry.

"This is his brother, Mart.

"This is Jack Penn, Jack Beechum Penn.

"This is Flora Catlett, my other daughter-in-law.

"This is my son, Andy.

"You know Henry.

"This is Lyda Branch, Danny's wife.

"This is Hannah Coulter.

"And this is Hannah's husband, Nathan."

One by one, they silently held out their hands to Kyle Bode, who silently shook them.

He and Wheeler had come almost all the way around the room. There was a single chair against the wall to the left of the door to Wheeler's office. Wheeler offered this chair, with a gesture, to Kyle Bode, who thanked him and sat down. Wheeler then seated himself in the chair between Hilda Roe's desk and the stair door.

"Mr. Bode," Wheeler said. "All of us here are relatives or friends of Burley Coulter."

The secretary, Kyle Bode noticed, now began to write in shorthand on her pad. It was noon and past, and he had learned nothing that he could tell to any superior or any reporter who might ask.

"Nathan," Wheeler went on, "is Burley's nephew."

"Nephew?" Kyle Bode said, turning to Nathan, who looked back at him with a look that was utterly direct and impenetrable.

"That's right."

"I assume you know him well."

"I've known him for fifty-three years."

"You've been neighbors that long?"

"I was raised by his parents and by him. We've been neighbors ever since, except for a while back there in the forties when I was away."

"You were in the service?"

"Yes."

The detective coughed. "Mr. Coulter, my job, I guess, is to find your uncle. Do *you* know where he is? Or where Danny Branch is?"

The eyes that confronted him did not look down, nor did they change. And there was no apparent animosity in the reply: "I couldn't rightly say I do."

"Now them two was a pair," Mart Rowanberry said, as though he were not interrupting but merely contributing to the conversation. "There's been a many a time when nobody knew where them two was."

"I see. And why was that?"

"They're hunters!" Art Rowanberry said, a little impatiently, in the tone of one explaining the obvious. "They'd be off somewheres in the woods."

"A many a time," Mart said, "he has called me out after bedtime to go with him, and I would get up and go. A many a time."

"You are friends, then, you and Mr. Coulter?"

"We been friends, you might as well say, all along. Course, now, he's older than I am. Fifteen years or so, wouldn't it be, Andy?"

The Catlett by the name of Andy nodded, and Lyda said, "Yes."

And then she said, "You knew him all your life, and then finally he didn't know you, did he, Mart?"

"He didn't know you?" said Kyle Bode.

"Well, sir," Mart said, "I come up on him and Danny and Nathan while they was fencing. Burley was asleep, propped up against the end post. I shook him a little, and he looked up. He says, 'Howdy, old bud.' I seen he was bewildered. I says, 'You don't know me, do you?' He says, 'I know I ought to, but I don't.' I says, 'Well, if you was to hear old Bet open up on a track, who'd you say it was?' And he says, 'Why, hello, Mart!' "

There was a moment then in which nobody spoke, as if everybody there was seeing what Mart had told.

Kyle Bode waited for that moment to pass, and then he said, "This Bet you spoke of"—he knew he was a fool, but he wanted to know—"was she a dog?" It was not his conversation he was in; he could hardly think by what right he was in it.

"She was a blue tick mostly," Mart said. "A light, sort of cloudy-colored dog, with black ears and a white tip to her tail. And a good one." He paused, perhaps seeing the dog again. "I bought her from Braymer Hardy over yonder by Goforth. But I expect," he said, smiling at Kyle Bode, "that was before your time." And then, as if conscious of having strayed from the subject, he said,

"But, now, Burley Coulter. They never come no finer than Burley Coulter."

Another small silence followed, in which everybody assented to Mart's tribute.

"Burley Coulter," Wheeler said, "was born in 1895. He was the son of Dave and Zelma Coulter. He had one older brother, Jarrat, who died in the July of 1967.

"Burley attended the Goforth School as long as he could be kept there—not long enough for him to finish the eighth grade, which he thought might have taken him forever. His fame at Willow Hole was not for scholarship but for being able to fight as well on the bottom as on the top."

Wheeler spoke at first to Kyle Bode. And then he looked down at his hands and thought a minute. When he spoke again, he spoke to and for them all.

"He was wild, Burley was, as a young fellow. For me, he had all the charm of an older boy who was fine looking and wild and friendly to a younger cousin. I loved him and would have followed him anywhere. Though he was wild, he didn't steal or lie or misrepresent himself.

"He never was a gambler. Once I said to him, 'Burley, I know you've drunk and fought and laid out at night in the woods. How come you've never gambled?' And he said, 'No son of a bitch is going to snap his fingers and pick up *my* money.' I said, 'Why?' And he said, 'Because I never got it by snapping my fingers.'

"His wildness was in his refusal, or his inability, to live within other people's expectations. He would be hunting sometimes when his daddy wanted him at work.

He would dance all night and neglect to sober up before he came home.

"He was called into the army during the First World War. By then he was past twenty and long past being a boy, and he had his limits. He hit an officer for calling him a stupid, briar-jumping Kentucky bastard. He might have suffered any one of those insults, if given singly. But he felt that, given all together, they paid off any obligation he had to the officer, and he hit him. He hit him, as he said, 'thoroughly.' I asked him, 'How thoroughly?' And he said, 'Thoroughly enough.' They locked him up a while for that.

"He was acting, by then, as a man of conscious principle. He didn't believe that anybody had the right, by birth or appointment, to lord it over anybody else.

"He broke his mother's heart, as she would sometimes say—as a young man of that kind is apt to do. But when she was old and only the two of them were left at home, he was devoted to her and took dutiful care of her, and she learned to depend on him.

"Though he never gave up his love of roaming about, he had become a different man from the one he started out to be. I'm not sure when that change began. Maybe it was when Nathan and Tom started following him around when they were little boys, after their mother died. And then, when Danny came along, Burley took his proper part in raising him. He took care of his mother until she died. He was a good and loyal partner to his brother. He was a true friend to all his friends.

"He was too late, as he thought and said, in acknowledging Danny as his son. But he did acknowledge him, and made him his heir, and brought him and Lyda home with him to live. And so at last he fully honored his should-have-been marriage to Kate Helen.

"He and I had our differences. Sometimes they came to words, and when they did I always learned something from him—a hard lesson sometimes, but good to know—because he knew himself and he told the truth.

"He was sometimes, but never much in a public way, a fiddler. And he was always a singer. His head was full of scraps and bits of songs that he sang out at work to say how he felt or to make himself feel better. Some of them, I think, he made up himself.

"From some morning a long time ago, I remember standing beside a field where Burley was plowing with a team of mules and hearing his voice all of a sudden lift up into the quiet:

> *Ain't going to be much longer, boys,*
> *Ain't going to be much longer.*
> *Soon it will be dinnertime*
> *And we will feed our hunger.*

And he had another song he sometimes sang up in the afternoon, when the day had got long and he was getting tired:

> *Look down that row;*
> *See how far we've got to go.*
> *It's a long time to sundown, boys,*
> *Long time to sundown.*

"What was best in him, maybe, was the pleasure he took in pleasurable things. We'll not forget his laughter. He was hunting once for two or three days. When he got home he was half starved, and it was the middle of the night. Rather than disturb the house, he went to the smokehouse and sliced part of a cured bacon with his pocketknife and ate it as it was. He said, 'I *relished* it.' He looked at the world and found it good.

" 'I've never learned anything until I had to,' he often said, and so confessed himself a man like other men. But he learned what he had to, and he changed, and so he made himself exceptional.

"He was, I will say, a faithful man."

It was a lonely gathering for Henry Catlett. He was riding as an humble passenger in a vehicle that he ought to have been guiding—that would not be guided if he did not guide it—and yet he had no better idea than the others where it might be going.

So far, he thought, he had done pretty well. He had gathered all parties to the case—except, of course, for the principals—here under his eye for the time being. How long he would need to keep them here or how long the various ones of them would stay, he did not know. He knew that Lyda had left a note for Danny where he would see it when he came home, telling him to join them here. But when Danny might come home, Henry did not know. Nobody, anyhow, had said anything about eating dinner, though it was past noon, and he was grateful for that.

Either he would be able to keep them there long enough, or he would not. Either Danny would show up, or he would not—wearing, or not wearing, that very regrettable blue shirt. At moments, as in a bad dream, he had wondered what it would portend if Danny showed up with fresh earth caked on his shoes. He wondered what concatenation of circumstances and lucky guesses might give Detective Bode some purchase on his case. It occurred to Henry to wish that Danny had given somebody a little notice of what he was going to do. But if Danny had been the kind of man to give such notice, he would not have done what he had done. It did not occur to Henry to regret that Danny had done what he had done.

As Wheeler spoke, his auditors sat looking at him, or down at their hands, or at the floor. From time to time, tears shone in the eyes of one or another of them. But no tear fell, no hand was lifted, no sound was uttered. And Henry was grateful to them all—grateful to his father, who was presuming on his seniority to keep them there; grateful to the others for their disciplined and decorous silence.

Out the corner of his eye, Henry could see his brother, Andy, slouched in his chair in the corner and watching also. Henry would have given a lot for a few minutes of talk with Andy. They would not need to say much.

Henry would have liked, too, to know what Lyda thought, and Hannah and Nathan. But though he sat in the same room with them, he was divided from them as by a wide river. All he could do was wait and watch.

And without looking directly at him, he watched Kyle

Bode, partly with amusement. The detective's questions to Nathan and to Mart and now his attention to Wheeler so obviously exceeded his professional interest in the case that something like a grin occurred in Henry's mind, though his face remained solemn.

"He was, I will say, a faithful man," Wheeler said.

And then Henry heard the street door open and slow footsteps start up the stairs.

Wheeler heard them, too, and stopped. Kyle Bode heard them; glancing around the room, he saw that all of them were listening. He saw that Lyda and Hannah were holding hands. Silence went over the whole room now and sealed them under it, as under a stone.

The footsteps rose slowly up the stairs, crossed the narrow hallway, hesitated a moment at the door. And then the knob turned, the door opened, and Danny Branch stepped into the room, wearing a shirt green as the woods, his well-oiled shoes as clean as his cap. He was smiling. To those seated around the book-lined old walls, he had the aspect and the brightness of one who had borne the dead to the grave, and filled the grave to the brim, and received the dead back into life again. The knuckles of Lyda's and Hannah's interlaced fingers were white; nobody made a sound.

And then Henry, whose mind seemed to him to have been racing a long time to arrive again there in the room, which now was changed, said quietly, "Well, looks like you made it home from Indiana."

And suddenly Kyle Bode was on his feet, shouting at

Danny, as if from somewhere far outside that quiet room. "Where *have* you been? What have you done with him? He's dead, isn't he, and you have buried him somewhere in these end-of-nowhere, godforsaken hills and hollows?"

"I had an account to settle with one of my creditors," Danny said, still smiling, to Kyle Bode.

"Sit down, Mr. Bode," Henry said, still quietly. "You don't have the right to ask him anything. Before you have that right, you have got to have evidence. And you haven't got a nickel's worth. You haven't got any."

The room was all ashimmer now with its quiet. There was a strangely burdening weight in Kyle Bode that swayed him toward that room and what had happened in it. He saw his defeat, and he was not even sorry. He felt small and lost, somewhere beyond the law. He sat down.

Henry watched him until he had fully subsided in his chair, and then went on:

"A man has disappeared out of your world, Mr. Bode, that he was never in for very long. And you don't know where, and you don't know how. He has disappeared into his people and his place, not to be found in this world again forever."

"And so," Wheeler said, after the room had again regained its silence, "peace to our neighbor, Burley Coulter. May God rest his soul."

5

Are You All Right?

The spring work had started, and I needed a long night's rest, or that was my opinion, and I was about to go to bed, but then the telephone rang. It was Elton. He had been getting ready for bed, too, I think, and it had occurred to him then that he was worried.

"Andy, when did you see the Rowanberrys?"

I knew what he had on his mind. The river was in flood. The backwater was over the bottoms, and Art and Mart would not be able to get out except by boat or on foot.

"Not since the river came up."

"Well, neither have I. And their phone's out. Mary, when did Mart call up here?"

I heard Mary telling him, "Monday night," and then, "It was Monday night," Elton said to me. "I've tried to call every day since, and I can't get anybody. That's four days."

"Well, surely they're all right."

"Well, that's what Mary and I have been saying. Surely they are. They've been taking care of themselves a long time. But, then, you never know."

"The thing is, we *don't* know."

We knew what we were doing, and both of us were a little embarrassed about it. The Rowanberry Place had carried that name since the first deeds were recorded in the log cabin that was the first courthouse at Hargrave. Rowanberrys had been taking care of themselves there for the better part of two hundred years. We knew that Arthur and Martin Rowanberry required as little worrying about as anybody alive. But now, in venturing to worry about them, we had put them, so to speak, under the sign of mortality. They were, after all, the last of the Rowanberrys, and they were getting old. We were uneasy in being divided from them by the risen water and out of touch. It caused us to think of things that could happen.

Elton said, "It's not hard, you know, to think of things that could happen."

"Well," I said, "do you think we'd better go see about them?"

He laughed. "Well, we've thought, haven't we? I guess we'd better go."

"All right. I'll meet you at the mailbox."

I hung up and went to get my cap and jacket.

"Nobody's heard from Art and Mart for four days," I said to Flora. "Their phone's out."

"And you and Elton are going to see about them," Flora said. She had been eavesdropping.

"I guess we are."

Flora was inclined to be amused at the way Elton and I imagined the worst. She did not imagine the worst. She just dealt with mortality as it happened.

I picked up a flashlight as I went out the door, but it was not much needed. The moon was big, bright enough to put out most of the stars. I walked out to the mailbox and made myself comfortable, leaning against it. Elton and I had obliged ourselves to worry about the Rowanberrys, but I was glad all the same for the excuse to be out. The night was still, the country all silvery with moonlight, inlaid with bottomless shadows, and the air shimmered with the trilling of peepers from every stream and pond margin for miles, one full-throated sound filling the ears so that it seemed impossible that you could hear anything else.

And yet I heard Elton's pickup while it was still a long way off, and then light glowed in the air, and then I could see his headlights. He turned into the lane and stopped and pushed the door open for me. I made room for myself among a bundle of empty feed sacks, two buckets, and a chain saw.

"Fine night," he said. He had lit a cigarette, and the cab was fragrant with smoke.

"It couldn't be better, could it?"

"Well, the moon could be just a little brighter, and it could be a teensy bit warmer."

I could hear that he was grinning. He was in one of his companionable moods, making fun of himself.

I laughed, and we rode without talking up out of the Katy's Branch valley and turned onto the state road.

"It's awful the things that can get into your mind," Elton said. "I'd hate it if anything was to happen to them."

The Rowanberrys were Elton's friends, and because they were his, they were mine. Elton had known them ever since he was just a little half-orphan boy, living with his mother and older brothers on the next farm up the creek. He had got a lot of his raising by being underfoot and in the way at the Rowanberrys'. And in the time of his manhood, the Rowanberry Place had been one of his resting places.

Elton worked hard and worried hard, and he was often in need of rest. But he had a restless mind, which meant that he could not rest on his own place in the presence of his own work. If he rested there, first he would begin to think about what he had to do, and then he would begin to do it.

To rest, he needed to be in somebody else's place. We spent a lot of Sunday afternoons down at the Rowanberrys', on the porch looking out into the little valley in the summertime, inside by the stove if it was winter. Art and Mart batched there together after their mother died, and in spite of the electric lights and telephone and a few machines, they lived a life that would have been recognizable to Elias Rowanberry, who had marked his X in the county's first deed book—a life that involved hunting and fishing and foraging as conventionally as it involved farming. They practiced an old-fashioned independence, an old-fashioned generosity, and an old-fashioned fidelity to their word and their friends. And they were hound men of the old correct school. They would not let a dog tree anywhere in earshot, day or night, workday or Sunday, without going to him. "It can be a nuisance," Art said, "but it don't hardly seem right to disappoint 'em."

Mart was the one Elton liked best to work with. Mart was not only a fine hand but had a gift for accommodating himself to the rhythms and ways of his partner. "He can think your thoughts," Elton said. Between the two of them was a sympathy of body and mind that they had worked out and that they trusted with an unshaken, unspoken trust. And so Elton was always at ease and quiet in Mart's company when they were at rest.

Art was the rememberer. He knew what he knew and what had been known by a lot of dead kinfolks and neighbors. They lived on in his mind and spoke there, reminding him and us of things that needed to be remembered. Art had a compound mind, as a daisy has a compound flower, and his mind had something of the unwary comeliness of a daisy. Something that happened would remind him of something that he remembered, which would remind him of something that his grandfather remembered. It was not that he "lived in his mind." He lived in the place, but the place was where the memories were, and he walked among them, tracing them out over the living ground. That was why we loved him.

We followed the state road along the ridges toward Port William and then at the edge of town turned down the Sand Ripple Road. We went down the hill through the woods, and as we came near the floor of the valley,

Elton went more carefully and we began to watch. We crossed a little board culvert that rattled under the wheels, eased around a bend, and there was the backwater, the headlights glancing off it into the treetops, the road disappearing into it.

Elton stopped the truck. He turned off his headlights and the engine, and the quietness of the moonlight and the woods came down around us. I could hear the peepers again. It was wonderful what the road going under the water did to that place. It was not only that we could not go where we were used to going; it was as if a thought that we were used to thinking could not be thought.

"Listen!" Elton said. He had heard a barred owl off in the woods. He quietly rolled the window down.

And then, right overhead, an owl answered: "HOOOOOAWWW!"

And the far one said, "Hoo hoo hoohooaw!"

"Listen!" Elton said again. He was whispering.

The owls went through their whole repertory of hoots and clucks and cackles and gobbles.

"Listen to them!" Elton said. "They've got a lot on their minds." Being in the woods at night excited him. He was a hunter. And we were excited by the flood's interruption of the road. The rising of the wild water had moved us back in time.

Elton quietly opened his door and got out and then, instead of slamming the door, just pushed it to. I did the same and came around and followed him as he walked slowly down the road, looking for a place to climb out of the cut.

Once we had climbed the bank and stepped over the

fence and were walking among the big trees, we seemed already miles from the truck. The water gleamed over the bottomlands below us on our right; you could not see that there had ever been a road in that place. I followed Elton along the slope through the trees. Neither of us thought to use a flashlight, though we each had one, nor did we talk. The moon gave plenty of light. We could see everything—underfoot the blooms of twinleaf, bloodroot, rue anemone, the little stars of spring beauties, and overhead the littlest branches, even the blooms on the sugar maples. The ground was soft from the rain, and we hardly made a sound. The flowers around us seemed to float in the shadows so that we walked like waders among stars, uncertain how far down to put our feet. And over the broad shine of the backwater, the calling of the peepers rose like another flood, higher than the water flood, and thrilled and trembled in the air.

It was a long walk because we had to go around the inlets of the backwater that lay in every swag and hollow. Way off, now and again, we could hear the owls. Once we startled a deer and stood still while it plunged away into the shadows. And always we were walking among flowers. I wanted to keep thinking that they were like stars, but after a while I could not think so. They were not like stars. They did not have that hard, distant glitter. And yet in their pale, peaceful way, they shone. They collected their little share of light and gave it back. Now and then, when we came to an especially thick patch of them, Elton would point. Or he would raise his hand and we would stop a minute and listen to the owls.

I was wider awake than I had been since morning. I

would have been glad to go on walking all night long. Around us we could feel the year coming, as strong and wide and irresistible as a wind.

But we were thinking, too, of the Rowanberrys. That we were in a mood to loiter and did not loiter would have reminded us of them, if we had needed reminding. To go to their house, with the water up, would have required a long walk from any place we could have started. We were taking the shortest way, which left us with the problem that it was going to be a little too short. The best we could do, this way, would be to come down the valley until we would be across from the house but still divided from it by a quarter mile or more of back-water. We could call to them from there. But what if we got no answer? What if the answer was trouble? Well, they had a boat over there. If they needed us, one of them could set us over in the boat. But what if we got no answer? What if, to put the best construction upon silence, they could not hear us? Well, we could only go as near as we could get and call.

So if our walk had the feeling of a ramble, it was not one. We were going as straight to the Rowanberrys' house as the water and the lay of the land would allow. After a while we began to expect to see a light. And then we began to wonder if there was a light to see.

Elton stopped. "I thought we'd have seen their light by now."

I said, "They're probably asleep."

Those were the first words we had spoken since we left the truck. After so long, in so much quiet, our voices sounded small.

Elton went on among the trees and the shadows, and I followed him. We climbed over a little shoulder of the slope then and saw one window shining. It was the light of an oil lamp, so their electricity was out, too.

"And now we're found," Elton said. He sang it, just that much of the old hymn, almost in a whisper.

We went through a little more of the woods and climbed the fence into the Rowanberrys' hill pasture. We could see their big barn standing up black now against the moonlight on the other side of the road, which was on high ground at that place, clear of the backwater.

When we were on the gravel we could hear our steps. We walked side by side, Elton in one wheel track, I in the other, until the road went under the water again. We were as close to the house then as we could get without a boat. We stopped and considered the distance.

And then Elton cupped his hands around his mouth, and called, "Ohhhhh, Mart! Ohhhhh, Art!"

We waited, it seemed, while Art had time to say, "Did you hear somebody?" and Mart to answer, "Well, I *thought* so." We saw light come to another window, as somebody picked up a lamp and opened the hall door. We heard the front door open. And then Art's voice came across the water: "Yeeeaaah?"

And Elton called back, "Are you aaalll riiight?"

I knew they were. They were all right, and we were free to go back through the woods and home to sleep.

But now I know that it was neither of the Rowanberrys who was under the sign of mortality that night. It was Elton. Before another April came he would be in his grave on the hill at Port William. Old Art Rowanberry, who had held him on his lap, would survive him by a dozen years.

And now that both of them are dead, I love to think of them standing with the shining backwater between them, while Elton's voice goes out across the distance, is heard and answered, and the other voice travels back: "Yeeeaaah!"

ABOUT THE AUTHOR

A native Kentuckian, Wendell Berry lived and taught in New York and California before returning permanently to the Kentucky River region. For the last three decades he has lived and farmed with his family on seventy-five acres in Henry County. He is a past fellow of both the Guggenheim Foundation and the Rockefeller Foundation, and is a former Stegner Fellow at Stanford University. He has received, among other awards, the Victory of Spirit Ethics Award in 1992 from the Louisville Community Foundation and the University of Louisville, and the Lannan Foundation Award for Nonfiction in 1989.

Author of more than two dozen books of fiction, poetry, and essays, Wendell Berry has been writing about the Port William membership in his novels and short stories for more than thirty years. Currently he lives and writes on his farm in Kentucky and teaches at the University of Kentucky.